CHECK OUT THE LIBRARY WEENIES

AND OTHER WARPED AND CREEPY TALES

STARSCAPE BOOKS BY DAVID LUBAR

CHECK OUT THE
LIBRARY
WEENIES

AND OTHER WARPED AND CREEPY TALES

DAVID LUBAR

A TOM DOHERTY ASSOCIATES BOOK
NEW YORK

CHECK OUT THE LIBRARY WEENIES:
AND OTHER WARPED AND CREEPY TALES

Copyright © 2018 by David Lubar

Reader's Guide copyright © 2018 by Tor Books

Emperor of the Universe excerpt copyright © 2018 by David Lubar
"A Boy and His Frog" originally appeared in *Ribbiting Tales*, edited by Nancy Springer. Story copyright © 2000 by David Lubar

A Starscape Book
Published by Tom Doherty Associates
175 Fifth Avenue
New York, NY 10010

www.tor-forge.com

The Library of Congress Cataloging-in-Publication Data is available upon request.

ISBN 978-0-7653-9706-5 (hardcover)
ISBN 978-0-7653-9708-9 (ebook)

Our books may be purchased in bulk for promotional, educational, or business use. Please contact your local bookseller or the Macmillan Corporate and Premium Sales Department at 1-800-221-7945, extension 5442, or by email at MacmillanSpecialMarkets@macmillan.com.

First Edition: September 2018

Printed in the United States of America

0 9 8 7 6 5 4 3 2 1

For Ed Masessa, a great guy with a big smile and a warm heart.
Thank you for giving the Weenies a wonderful second home.

CONTENTS

CONTENTS

CHECK OUT THE
LIBRARY
WEENIES
AND OTHER WARPED AND CREEPY TALES

HOW TO SLAY VAMPIRES
FOR FUN AND PROFIT

Johann was, at the moment, an unwilling patron of the Fedderville Public Library. His parents had dragged him there because they wanted to hear a local author speak about her trip to the South Pole. Johann had no interest in poles or local authors. He had no interest in books, either, until he spotted the faded gold letters on the faded brown spine of a thin volume jutting slightly from a shelf in a far-off dusty corner of the second floor of the library, where he'd wandered, looking for something to amuse himself. He read the title twice, since the first reading left him with the impression he'd misread the words. But no, they were just what they'd seemed on first glance: *How to Slay Vampires for Fun and Profit*.

Johann was always ready for fun. He was also in favor of profit. He pulled the book from between its shelf mates. *Somebody messed up*, he thought, as he noticed that the books on either side were volumes of poetry written by some guy named Byron. Obviously, the book had been misshelved. No matter. It was in his hands now. He sat on the floor and started reading. He was halfway through the book by the time his parents tracked him down. Their annoyance at having to hunt for him was balanced by their joy at seeing him enthralled by a book for the first time in his life. Both parents, upon reading the title, assumed it was a work of fiction.

Johann continued to read in the car. He finished the book that evening, sitting on the living room couch. He now knew how to lure vampires, trap them, slay them, and sell their ashes for an amazing sum. He'd vaguely known that slain vampires disintegrated into ashes, but he'd no idea there was a market for those powdery remains. The book listed the addresses of several places that would buy them, and Johann checked the Internet to make sure those places were real.

Since the task of slaying vampires was not a solo occupation, Johann enlisted the aid of his friends Cameron and Luis. He told them all about the fun they'd have, but he didn't mention the profit. That money would be all his.

Cameron and Luis shared Johann's dark nature, so they were easily persuaded to join the venture. It helped that Luis had a supply of sparklers left over from the Fourth of July. Those were an important component in the slaying part. Their burning light, apparently, could transfix a vampire once several common chemicals were added to the existing mix. It also helped that Cameron's father was a passionate gardener, with a fondness for the larger varieties of tomatoes. Heavy duty tomato stakes were easily converted into weapons for plunging into vampire hearts.

Throughout the preparation phase, Johann searched all around the town, and all across any countryside within range of a lazy bicyclist, for a site to which he could lure the vampires. The book stated that three to five victims was a reasonable number to expect, though there had been reports of slayers harvesting as many as a dozen. Johann knew he'd do well above average.

Fortunately, human blood was not required to bait the trap, though Johann was pretty sure he could convince Cameron to donate a small quantity if he egged him on with taunts about cowardice. Cameron was easily manipulated. But his blood wouldn't be needed. According to the book, fresh beef would do, mixed with an assortment of herbs and spices that were not difficult to obtain. Johann chose the middle school gym for the site of the slaughter, because he knew how to get inside the building, even when it was supposed to be locked.

Once the vampire slayers reached the gym, they set out the bait in the darkened, cavernous room. Johann opened the book to the spot he'd marked, illuminated the page with his phone, and read the chant that would help lure the vampires.

As the last word died in the darkness, the vampires came. Silent, half human in form, half smoke, they entered the gym. Five! Then six! Then seven! Then eight! Male and female, they approached the bucket. Johann held his breath, hoping those drawn by the chant and the scent would exceed the dozen mentioned in the book. Soon enough, they did. A dozen came, followed by two more. And then, a final straggler arrived. There were fifteen in all, now fully solidified from their smoke-edged transitionary bodies, forming a ring around the bait in its bucket on the floor, staring down, as if waiting for a command.

It's a record! Johann's mind flashed between thoughts of fame and thoughts of riches. Both would be his. Maybe he could even write his own book.

Flanking him, Luis and Cameron trembled visibly. Not Johann. He felt steely calm, and eager to get started. The book was true to its promise. This would be fun. He hefted the plastic bag that lay at his feet, savoring the weight of the stakes and picturing the thrilling leap into action that would mark the start of the slaying. He would move through the vampires like a hero in a blockbuster movie, skewering their undead hearts.

"Light it," Johann whispered to Luis, when it seemed likely no more vampires would arrive. The first sparkler, specially prepared to ignite easily, hissed like a serpent and threw glowing sparks that pierced the darkness. Luis lit two more sparklers from the first one, and handed them to his fellow vampire slayers.

Johann tucked the book under his arm and raised his sparkler. "Yield!" he shouted, approaching the vampires. "Kneel before me!"

One vampire knelt, just as the book had described. He bowed his head and said, "Yes, my master. I will do your bidding."

Master! Johann loved the feeling of power the word sent through his body.

The vampire next to the kneeling one smacked him on the shoulder. The kneeling vampire rose. "I was just messing with him," he said.

The vampires laughed. The sound struck Johann like a stab to the gut.

"Sparklers . . . ," one of the vampires said. "How could anybody believe something so ridiculous?"

Johann felt more stabs of fear. This time, the jabs pierced his lungs.

"How could anybody believe we could be trapped?" a vampire to Johann's left said. "What fools these mortals be!"

"Oh, that's original," a shorter vampire said in a mocking tone.

This set off a round of chatter.

"Kneel!" Johann shouted, not yet understanding that he was the one who'd been hunted, lured, and trapped. Though he'd been caught with bait far more devious and subtle than a slab of beef dripping with cow's blood. He took a step forward. Luis and Cameron remained frozen where they stood, clutching their useless sparklers.

Instead of kneeling, the vampires leaped onto their victims. It was their turn for fun, and for feasting. As Johann's life drained away, the book slipped from beneath his arm.

A vampire snatched it before it could hit the floor.

The vampire who had knelt picked up a dying sparkler and waved it in a figure eight. "I used to love these things."

"Me, too," another said.

After the feast, the vampires, half smoke again, and half undead flesh, drifted away from the gym. One of them carried the book to another library, in another town, for the next clueless fun seeker to find. Because, whether you're a human or a vampire, it's nice, sometimes, to get your meal delivered.

COME BACK SOON

'm a total failure," Dad said. He slumped to the floor of the garage—which also served as his lab—and drooped his head like he was offering his neck to an executioner. "I've let the whole family down, Bianca. I wouldn't blame you if you abandoned me."

Dad has a bit of a dramatic side. That's okay. Everyone has flaws. But he's super smart. He's a genius, actually. I knew he'd been working on a top secret invention. He'd kept hinting that he was about to reveal it, and dazzle the world. He'd actually invented some pretty cool things, but nothing that could really be called dazzling. Still, it was awesome that he could come up with ideas for things that didn't exist.

I'd been hanging out in the driveway, keeping an eye on my little brother, Tyler, who was pedaling his tricycle in wobbly circles, but I'd gone inside when Dad let out the sigh that came before his cry of despair. I sat on the floor next to him, slumped my own head parallel with his, and then turned it so we were face-to-face. Or, actually, face to side of face.

"Tell me about it," I said.

Dad reached up, fumbled around for a second in a box at the edge of the work bench behind him, then plucked something out. "This is what I've spent the last six months working on," he said.

I studied the object in his hand. It was a clear disk of plastic, about twice the size of a silver dollar. I could see thin lines etched in it, like electronic circuits, and a tiny silvery disk in the center that might have been a battery. "It's pretty," I said.

"It's a failure," he said.

I waited for more information, but he remained silent and sad. Finally, I asked, "What does it do?"

"It's supposed to be a time machine," he said.

Now he really had my full attention. "That's pretty awesome." I pictured myself leaping back through the centuries to have a conversation with Martha Washington or Joan of Arc.

"It would be, if it worked," he said.

I had to agree with that. And I guess I understood why Dad was moping. I tried to decide whether to suggest ice cream or a trip to the park. Both had the ability to cheer Dad up. As I was looking for a way to combine those things, even though they were in different directions, Dad said, "What good is it to go back such a short distance, and so briefly?"

I'm embarrassed to say it took me a moment to realize what I'd just heard.

"Wait!" I shouted, when the meaning of Dad's words hit me. He hadn't failed. He'd succeeded. "You can travel through time! That's amazing."

"Fifteen seconds," he said. "Maybe I can get it up to twenty, if I put in another month's work. But the fabric of time is too resilient to allow for traveling farther into the past than that.

It's like jumping off a cliff when you're tied to a very short bungee cord. You travel a brief distance, and then you snap right back. I thought I could figure a way around it, and travel decades, or even centuries, into the past. But everything I tried has failed. I just can't get beyond that limit. And you can only stay in the past for about five seconds."

"Dad!" I said, grabbing his shoulder. "You invented time travel!"

I said it again, shouting the words, as if a higher volume would break through the wall of gloom he'd erected. "Tyler!" I shouted at my brother. "Dad invented time travel!"

Tyler didn't seem impressed. "Watch me!" he shouted back as he pedaled past the open door of the garage.

"In a minute." I turned my attention back to Dad.

"A minute," Dad said, echoing my words. "I can't even go that far."

"Can I try it?" I asked.

"Sure. It's safe. I tested it pretty thoroughly." He leaned over and placed the disk on the floor. "Step on it with either foot."

I got up and placed my right foot on the disk. It made a sound between a hum and a whoosh. And then, as the sound faded, I leaped back in time, to a quarter minute earlier. I didn't feel anything strange. Not at first. It wasn't like flying or falling. Time travel, itself, didn't produce any sensations.

The realization that I'd traveled back to where I'd been, on the other hand, hit me pretty hard. I saw myself sitting there, talking to Dad. My jaw dropped, and my stomach felt as if I'd just swallowed emptiness. I was standing in the past, watching myself! But by the time I focused on the scene in front of me, and accepted that I'd traveled through time, I'd snapped back to the present.

"That was . . . it was . . . ," I stumbled around, searching for a way to describe the experience, and finally settled for, "Whoa!"

"Unfortunately, that's about as impressive as it gets," Dad said.

Something puzzling popped into my mind. "How come the me who was sitting there didn't see the me who'd traveled back in time?"

"Because, for the you who was sitting there, the you who traveled hadn't traveled yet," Dad said.

"That doesn't make any sense."

"Welcome to time travel," Dad said. "It's senseless and limited. I can't believe I spent so much time working on it."

One corner of his lips twitched, like he was close to smiling. I guess he realized it was strange to talk about time spent working on time travel. But then, his face grew sad again.

There had to be more to his invention than that. I stepped off the disk. "Can I do it again?" I wanted to take another look at the recent past.

"It's reusable," Dad said.

The second time, I was prepared for the shock of transition, and turned all my attention to watching the scene in front of me. It was slightly later than before. That made sense, because I'd also jumped back from a slightly later time.

I was less disoriented on this trip. But I was a whole lot more awestruck on my return. It didn't matter how long it lasted, or how far you could go. *My dad had invented time travel!* I'd bet a lot of really smart scientists believed that was impossible.

I needed to convince Dad to stop being so hard on himself, and get back to work. There had to be a way he could turn this into a useful invention. But that couldn't happen while he was moping and feeling like a failure.

As I opened my mouth, I heard the horrible screech of brakes. Not car brakes. These were ear-wrenching truck brakes that sounded like the shriek of a mechanical monster yanking out one of its own ribs.

"Tyler!" Dad and I both shouted.

I looked out at the driveway, my heart jamming itself half-way up my throat. Tyler wasn't there. We ran to the street, and saw something that yanked my heart the rest of the way up my throat and flung it far away. Tyler and his tricycle were crumpled into a mangled mess in front of the truck.

"No!" Dad raced toward him.

This was all my fault. I was supposed to be watching him. I had to fix things. I sped back to the garage and grabbed one of Dad's time machines. Then, I threw the disk out the garage door onto the driveway. Gasping for breath, I rushed outside and stepped on the disk, desperate to save my little brother. I'd throw myself between him and the truck, if I had to.

I went back in time, but not far enough. The accident had already happened, more than fifteen seconds ago.

"No!" I shouted. I couldn't let things end up this way. I had the power to go back in time. Somehow, I had to be able to use that to save Tyler.

I staggered as a powerful idea hit me. It was outrageous. But it had to work.

As Dad knelt by my brother, and the truck driver opened his door, I ran, again, into the garage. This time, I grabbed the whole box of disks. I dropped one on the floor, right in front of me, and stepped on it.

The instant I arrived fifteen seconds into my past, I tossed down another disk, one giant step ahead of me. Before I could snap back to the present, I jumped onto the second disk. If I was right, I was now almost half a minute into the past, not counting the time it took to move to the second disk. I wanted to glance outside, but I knew I just had a few seconds to make my next leap. I tossed another disk, and stepped on that one. And another, moving as far as I dared with each disk, making my way to the driveway. I heard the screech of brakes, again. I'd reached that first terrible moment. But I had to go back even farther. I ignored the sound and kept tossing disks. And I kept listening for what I needed.

Finally, I heard tricycle wheels on the street in front of me. I tossed another disk.

I heard tricycle wheels in the driveway!

It worked!

I tossed three more disks, one at a time, moving forward a few feet in space and backward almost fifteen seconds in time with each hop. Finally, I reached the point where Tyler was still pedaling in circles around the driveway. I made a guess about where he'd been fifteen seconds before that, threw the disk there, and stepped on it.

My guess was good. I traveled to a spot right next to him.

Now what?

There was no time to think. I pushed him off the tricycle, onto the grass. Then, I grabbed the handlebar, twisted my upper body, and flung the tricycle as far and as hard as I could, like an Olympic hammer thrower.

As the tricycle left my hands, I was jolted back to the present, in a series of hops.

Dizzy, disoriented, and out of breath, I was back where I'd

started when I'd stepped onto the disk in the garage, in my second attempt to save Tyler. But Dad was there, too. He was glaring at me as he delivered a lecture. Dad never yells at us, but he was coming pretty close to that right now. Not that I could blame him. As far as he knew, I'd just acted like the world's worst big sister and biggest bully.

Tyler, his face streaked with tears, was clutching Dad's leg.

"There had better be a good explanation for your actions," Dad said.

"There is," I said, after my trembling body had calmed down enough that I could grab a breath and talk. "A really good one."

I knew Dad would understand when I explained that I'd erased an unbearable tragedy from our lives. And I knew he'd be thrilled his time machine could be used to travel more than just a short hop into the past.

Before I could even start my explanation, he pointed to the box in my hand. "You did something with those disks."

"Yeah."

"Something major?"

"Definitely."

"Something best discussed over ice cream?" he asked.

"Absolutely."

"Then there's no point wasting time here," he said. "Let's go."

I told you he was a genius.

ALL THAT GLITTERS

Can you transform precious metals?" I asked the wizard when he opened the door of the modest hut near the outskirts of town. It had taken me three weeks of inquiries, bribes, and menacing stares to uncover his location, and half a week more to verify that the rumors about his abilities were most likely true. He looked ancient enough to have mastered an arcane skill or two over the years. That was good. I'd learned long ago that young wizards were unreliable, even if they were enthusiastic. They were more interested in showing you what they could do than in finding out what magic you needed them to perform.

"Transmutation is expensive," he said. "The cost of turning lead to gold, for example, would be greater than the value of the gold that was created." He shrugged, as if to say that this was why the world wasn't overflowing with wealthy wizards.

"I understand." I ignored his minor correction of my use of *transform*, and turned our discussion toward his own misinterpretation of my question. "I do not wish to transmute a base element into a precious one. I have much more closely related metals in mind. I wish to change silver into gold. Can you do that?"

"That is certainly less difficult. As you mentioned, they are close in nature." He paused and blinked, then added, "Though the cost would still be more expensive than the resulting gold."

"But you can do it?" I asked. Even old wizards needed to be approached with patience.

"I can do whatever you wish, as long as I am paid well enough. Where is this silver object? Did you bring it with you?" He swept his gaze across me, though I carried nothing.

I laughed at his second misconception. "It is not one item. It is all the items in a dwelling."

"An entire dwelling?" I saw his brief amazement replaced by a calculating smile and narrowed eyes. "That, my friend, would be extremely expensive."

"And very much worth it," I said, masking my delight. I knew that the more eager I appeared, the higher his price would be. "I wish to surprise a man who has played an important role in my life. I believe that turning all his silver into gold would provide an adequate and unique reward for the impact he has had on my life, and on the lives of many of my friends. There is nothing more precious than gold. He deserves this gift." I was talking mostly as a bargaining trick, knowing that it was best to try to get him to tell me the cost, rather than name one, myself. The smart buyer always waits to see what will satisfy the seller.

"Describe the contents," he said.

I named the essential items. His smile grew broader as the list grew longer. He told me his price. We haggled, because that is expected. I managed to reduce his extraordinarily expensive demand somewhat. It was still a huge sum. That didn't matter. My purse is deep. I would gladly have paid twice what he'd first asked. That's how important this was to me.

I shivered at the thought of Baron Trexler discovering my gift. He would be so surprised when he realized who was behind the transmutation.

"When can you do this?" I asked the wizard.

He glanced past me at the midday sky. "The spell works best at sunset, which is a powerful moment of transition. But transmutation requires light to fuel the change. The brighter the light, the purer the gold. Ideally, the spell should be cast when the moon is at its fullest."

"Can it be cast before then?" I asked. "I believe we are only at the half-moon, tonight."

"It can. But this is an instance when patience will be rewarded. The fuller the moon, the purer the gold. If you can't wait, the results will be less than perfect. But the price remains the same. The choice is yours."

"We'll wait," I said.

"You have made a wise choice," the wizard said. "There's just one more detail. I require full payment in advance."

"That is not a problem." I'd amassed a fortune before coming to seek the wizard, since I knew his fee would be high. One question remained. "And you can work this wizardry so it will be a surprise? I want to see the Baron's face when he discovers my gift."

"A wizard who lacks discretion is soon a dead wizard," he said. "Magic has claimed many foolish victims."

I gave him the location of Baron Trexler's home, and agreed

to arrange delivery of the funds. As I headed back to town, I heard the wizard mutter, "Thank goodness the world has so many fools like him, with full purses and empty heads."

I smiled, but didn't respond. I'm sure he assumed I was too far away to hear his words. And he didn't need to know how far from foolish my request was.

Fourteen days later, on the night of the transmutation, I met the wizard on a hillside within sight of the Baron's home. He'd brought a cart loaded with items both familiar and strange. I won't attempt to describe his actions, except that they involved a large mirror pointed at the home, a small cauldron filled with sweet-smelling herbs that smoldered on a bed of moss, and a scroll containing words in a language more foreign than any I'd encountered in my travels. The words had an ancient and powerful feel to them, as did his gestures.

The sunlight faded, replaced by moonlight.

"It is finished," the wizard said, just moments before the moon had fully risen.

"Good. You might want to flee. I can't guarantee your safety." Having done my best to spare the wizard from a terrible fate, I ran toward Baron Trexler's home. I was eager to reveal the marvelous twin surprises I had for him—my gift of gold and my presence.

My timing was perfect. The baron had just emerged from his front door, exactly as I had anticipated. He was dressed for the hunt—his chest and neck protected by a padded vest, his wrists banded with spiked bracelets, his rifle held ready for action.

I closed the distance, staying low and silent in the tall grass, barely rippling the wildflowers, getting near enough to see his face clearly before he spotted me. When he finally noticed my approach, he raised his rifle, showing no sign of surprise as he stared down the sight. It was those steel nerves that made him such a dangerous adversary.

I leaped. He fired. His aim was true. The bullet tore through my chest, and pierced the center of my heart. I felt it pass through my body, and exit my back.

He stepped aside, prepared, I suppose, for my leap to carry my corpse past him. I did fly past him, thanks to the force of my leap, but I was far from a corpse.

I turned toward him the instant I landed, now fully transformed. I snarled. It was an involuntary reaction to a deadly enemy, though none the less satisfying for being instinctual. He recovered quickly, despite the surprise. I, too, had recovered quickly. My heart and chest were fully healed.

He fired again. Another deadly shot. Deadly with a silver bullet. But not with one transmuted into gold. The hot metal passed through me without doing permanent damage.

I could have finished the game right then, slaying him on his doorstep as he fired golden bullets at me in vain, again and again. But he had hunted and killed my kind for decades. This was retribution time. Vengeance needed to be slow. I held off the urge to slay him where he stood in a flurry of rage. He tossed the empty rifle at me. I deflected it easily. He ran inside and dove for the fireplace, where he grabbed a sword from above the mantel. I held still as he swung a head-cleaving blow at me, making no effort to dodge or to deflect the attack, and howled in triumph as the soft gold of the blade bent beneath his fury but failed to sever my flesh or split my skull.

I slashed his shoulder with my claws, not yet cutting deeply enough to render that arm useless, then moved to block his attempt to escape through the front door. He grabbed a platter and hurled it at me like a discus thrower. I could have caught it and hurled it back, but I let it bounce harmlessly off my forehead, adding to the message at the center of this nightmare: *You can't hurt me, Baron. You are powerless.* I wanted his remaining moments to drown him in torrents of terror.

He ran from the room. I followed him into the kitchen. He grabbed a knife from a table, though by now I'm sure he had fully realized the futility of this.

I was only sorry I could not speak while I was in wolf form. It would have been fitting to tell him of all the lives he had ruined, naming the slain, one by one. I settled for letting my claws speak for me. They spoke slowly, throughout the time the full moon passed across the sky.

When dawn came, transforming me back to human form, I gathered the gold, and any other valuable items I could carry. I would need all of it to pay the next wizard. There were many hunters, in many lands, who deserved the same gift I'd given to Baron Trexler. And they would get it. Do unto others as they, themselves, have done to others. That was my golden rule.

BALD TRUTHS

Chemo stinks. Wait. I can think of a much better word for it than *stinks*. But it's the sort of word that would get me in trouble with my teacher. No. Actually, I would have to try extra hard to get in trouble these days. My teacher is very gentle about my feelings, because I have cancer. There are times when I catch her watching me with these really sad eyes. I think she's struggling not to cry, because teachers always have to be the bravest person in the room. It's probably harder for her to deal with my condition than it is for me. She's outside, looking at me. I'm inside, living with all the scary images and the big question marks. But, deep inside, I'm still just plain old Cindy Anne Selkirk. And, for a kid with cancer, I'm pretty lucky. I have the type of cancer that gets cured. Mine has what they call *a high remission rate*. That's a fancy way of saying I'm probably not going to die any time soon, thanks to the medicine they're giving me.

I started my chemotherapy last month. I felt kind of sick for a couple hours afterward, and pretty tired for two or three days, but it wasn't all that bad. I felt worse when I had the flu.

Or when I ate seven of my friend Debbie's mom's homemade buttermilk donuts. (I only did that once, since I'm capable of learning from my mistakes. After that, I never ate more than six donuts without taking a break.)

Anyhow, the doctors and nurses are giving me the medicine my body needs to kill the cancer. So, I'll be getting better. Eventually I won't be sick at all. Which is great. But my hair is starting to fall out. All of it. Even my eyebrows. Mom and Dad, and Dr. Polnower, who is totally awesome, warned me about it. I told them I didn't care. That was half a lie. I felt that I could make myself try to not care. And I'm sort of able to do that. But some of the kids in my class stare at me. And Billy Wechlington, who's always been a bully, whispers stuff when he thinks he can get away with it. He's called me *shinyhead, smooth-face,* and *cue-ball girl.* At least he's far meaner than he is clever. And I'll have the last laugh. My hair will grow back. He'll never grow up.

Still, it hurts when other kids make fun of me. I have to use up a lot of my strength and courage to make it through my treatment, and to fight the bad thoughts that try to sneak into my mind the same way the cancer invaded my body. There's not much energy left for battling against bullies.

Mom and Dad offered to buy me a wig. Any kind I wanted. Any style. Any color. That was very cool of them. And mom took me shopping for scarves I could wear on my head. But in my support group, some of the women talked about showing the world you don't care what they think. That's hard. But it's what I want to try to do. Though I have to admit, most of the wigs I've seen were pretty awesome. Maybe I'll get one after my hair grows back, just for fun.

I wasn't the only one, not counting the bullies, who was thinking about hair.

This afternoon, Debbie grabbed me as we were leaving school. "I have a great idea."

"Donuts?" I asked, though I wasn't really in the mood for one. My appetite was another victim of the chemo.

"I'm going to shave my head." She ran her hand through her beautiful beaded braids. "I'm going to ask everyone to do it."

"Why?" I knew the answer, but the question still slipped out.

"To show support for you," she said.

"But your hair is gorgeous," I said.

"*I'm* gorgeous." She flashed me a stunning smile and struck a sassy pose. "My hair just came along for the ride."

"It's not necessary," I said. "I can handle this. I'm fine."

"I know you are. You'd survive a zombie apocalypse all by yourself. You're the strongest girl I know, except around donuts. But that doesn't mean I don't need to do something for you. A lot of kids feel that way. This isn't really just for you. It's for me. It's for all of us. We want to do more than just tell you we care. We want to show you."

Right after Debbie said that, Billy brushed past me and muttered, "Shiny!"

"Not everyone." I grabbed Debbie's shoulder to keep her from chasing Billy down and thumping him. I could tell she wanted to knock that smirk off his face, and I'll admit I sort of wanted to see her do it, but I didn't want her to get in trouble. Our school has a pretty severe anti-thumping policy.

"Everyone who matters," Debbie said.

I think she was right about that. It's human nature to care

about other people. And I understood that the kids in my class wanted to help me. More importantly, I knew that stopping Debbie was way harder than stopping cancer. There was no cure, once she grabbed hold of an idea. There was no chemo strong enough to shut her down.

So she set things up, with some help from her parents, to make the haircuts a charity event. Kids and teachers who planned to shave their heads got their friends and relatives to pledge money. Even better, Debbie found out there was an organization that takes donated hair, if it's long enough, and uses it to make wigs for people with cancer.

The next thing I knew, mine was just one of many bald heads in our school, and in our classroom. When I walked down the hall at the start or the end of the school day, I felt like I'd been transported to a magical country that was both foreign and a long-lost home. It wasn't just my friends who shaved their heads. Some kids I didn't really know took part, too. So did the vice principal. Billy didn't do it, of course. Neither did the three kids who hung out with him. They even started coming to school each day with a different hair style. They'd gel it, or spike it, or hit it with the kind of spray-on color you can wash out. It didn't bother me at all. Or not all that much.

Okay, it bothered me, but I tried not to think about it.

Life went on. Chemo went on. My test results looked good. Dr. Polnower said I was responding well to the treatment. I missed four days of school in a row, because I was feeling pretty weak, but I made it back in time for our field trip to Limerock Caverns. That was great. I'd always wanted to go there.

We got picked up at the school parking lot pretty early, because it was a two-hour ride.

"I'm glad you made it," Debbie said when I joined her on the bus.

"Hey, slick," Billy said as he walked past me.

I notice he'd frizzed his hair out. So had his friends. I guess they wanted to make a special effort to mock me during the field trip.

I think I napped a little during the ride, but I was eager to get off the bus when we reached the caverns. And I had plenty of energy for the tour, which involved a lot of walking. The caverns were even more amazing than I'd imagined, with enormous stalactites and stalagmites that I pretended were monster teeth, and tiny, glittery crystals that looked like fairy treasures. I was buddied up with Debbie, of course. Most of our conversation involved single words that were all pretty much various ways of saying *Wow!*

After gazing our way through dozens of corridors and chambers, and even crossing over a small stream, we reached Doxley's Cathedral, the giant gorge at the heart of Limerock Caverns, named after the person who first explored the caves.

We gathered at a railing. The guide pressed a button, turning on dim lights that revealed the enormous rock formations and bottomless gap in front of us. He pressed another button, then pointed overhead. It took a moment for me to realize what we were looking at.

"Bats!" I said, more surprised than scared. I'm not super spooked by bats, but the ceiling of the chamber was pretty much a wall-to-wall carpet of flying mammals. Though they were sleeping, not flying, at the moment.

My shriek wasn't the loudest or the softest. Most of the group reacted with surprise. A few reacted with fear, but nobody seemed totally terrified. After we settled down, the guide said, "Don't worry. They're nocturnal. They won't leave the cave until sunset."

He was wrong.

The living carpet rippled. And then, it left the ceiling, morphing from a flat expanse of dark leather into a swirling orb that pulsed like a blob of black oil dropped into a vat of water.

The orb funneled toward us.

This time, all our screams were at full volume.

"Don't panic!" the guide screamed. "They won't attack people."

He was wrong again.

The bats attacked us.

We ran, screaming and flailing, for the exit. I felt I'd been dropped right into one of those escape sequences in a video game where you have to get out of a building that's burning and falling apart while a helicopter is shooting missiles at you, a mob of slobbering monsters is at your heels, and your controller is buzzing like a paper sack full of angry wasps. Okay, maybe it wasn't quite that bad, but it sure was close.

We burst from the cave and headed across the parking lot toward the safety of the bus. I was clutching Debbie's hand all the way to the bus as she pulled me along.

"Are you okay?" I asked when we got inside and tumbled into our seats. I was out of breath, and my heart was pounding, but I realized I hadn't felt this alive in months.

"Yeah," she said. "You?"

"I think so." I felt my head, and checked my arms. No bites or scratches. "Bats don't act like that," I said.

"Rabid bats would," Debbie said. Then, she gasped and

pointed out the bus window. I looked where she pointed, and gasped, too.

Billy stumbled out from the cavern. He had something on his head. Lots of things, actually.

"Bats," I said, as the creepy reality hit me. "He's covered with them."

"Bad hair day," Debbie said.

For sure. Or bat hair day. Billy had dozens of bats anchored in his hair. So did his friends, who emerged right after him. The bats were flapping their wings so frantically, I expected them to carry the bullies off. Eventually, Billy and the others swatted the bats out of their hair and got on the bus, crying, whimpering, and shaking so badly, I almost felt sorry for them. As a bonus, they were too traumatized to tease me at all during the ride home.

My parents took me for my final chemo that evening. Debbie's folks dropped her off at the hospital so she could meet me and ride home with us.

"Great day," she said when I saw her in the waiting area.

"Very great," I said.

Then her eyes got wide. She looked like she was about to scream.

"What's wrong?" I asked as she slapped her hand over her mouth. I was always a bit worn out after chemo, but Debbie had seen me like that before now. I wondered whether I looked worse than usual this time.

Her whole body was shaking.

"Is it that bad?" I asked.

She shook her head, spoke a muffled, "Nope," through her hand, and pointed past me with her other hand. When

I glanced over my shoulder, I realized she wasn't fighting against a scream. She was trying to keep from roaring with laughter.

So was I, when I saw who else was getting released. Though I felt a bit shocked, too, as I stared at Billy and his friends. They reminded me of extras from a low-budget zombie movie. Their heads had been shaved—I suppose to allow the doctors to treat the deep scratches and bites from the bats. All of them had needed stitches. I'd imagine they'd probably also gotten rabies shots and tons of antibiotics.

I guess I felt a bit sorry for them. But not sorry enough to resist saying, "Bald is beautiful," as they slinked past me.

"I'll bet this is one class trip they'll never forget," Debbie said.

"Especially after next Monday," I said. That was something I'd sort of been dreading for weeks, but now I was very eager for it.

"Right," Debbie said. "School photos. This is perfect."

And it was.

TOUGH CROWD

I **had five minutes** to live. No joke. And I was stuck in a room with seven kids who would have no problem letting me die. For that matter, they'd probably even volunteer to help me toward that exit, if they thought they could get away with it.

Everything would have worked out just fine if I hadn't gotten sent to lunch detention. I can get my friends rolling on the floor at my regular lunch table without even trying. I can almost always come up with a joke. Even if no good jokes pop into my mind, I can definitely get a laugh by doing something gross with my milk. But that wouldn't work here, in this windowless basement classroom. The detention crowd was basically made up of mean and angry brutes who hated kids like me at first sight. If you looked up "nerd" in the dictionary, my picture would be there, complete with taped-together eyeglasses and three pens in my shirt pocket. Unless one of the brutes had ripped the picture out, crumpled it up, and flushed it down the toilet.

Right after lunch started, Mr. Spalter, who was never supposed to leave us alone, dashed out. Probably for coffee. I knew it would be dangerous to attract attention in this room—I'd taken a seat off to one side and invested a lot of effort into breathing as quietly as possible—but I was desperate. I searched for the best killer line I could think of. And yeah, I noted the irony of using "killer" in a room filled with hostile slabs of flesh. It wasn't hard finding the perfect joke.

"Hey," I said, "did you hear the one about—"

"Shut up, jerk," Angus Loutman yelled. "Or I'll rip your head off and feed it to you."

I shut up, though it was hard to keep myself from pointing out the basic impossibility of what he'd threatened to do. It would have made more sense to threaten to shove my head down my throat, as opposed to feeding it to me. Still, in my experience, bullies don't like being corrected about the flawed logic of their threats, or anything else, for that matter.

The others laughed.

But that laughter didn't count. I hadn't made them laugh. Angus had.

My brain raced through my options. They were, as the old saying goes, slim and none. I had only one slender chance to make things work. And it wasn't a very good chance. I needed to try to get them to understand my situation, and have enough curiosity to let me explain what I needed.

"Listen!" I said, standing up and backing toward the corner until the walls stopped me from edging farther away.

Seven brutish heads rotated toward me. I saw three of my fellow detainees bracing themselves to rise from their desks. A fourth grabbed a book to throw at me.

I leaped into an explanation, hoping that my audience would be captivated by the weirdness of the story I was about to tell long enough for me to reach the finish. If not, I was really finished.

"I'll be dead in five minutes," I said, pointing to the clock over the door. "At noon, I will drop dead. Want to know why?"

This was the moment when everything could fail. I held my breath. It was always a risk to ask dangerous people a question. But it was also a good way to grab their attention. If my gamble failed, and they silenced me, either with words or with actions, it was over. Totally and horribly over in ways I didn't want to think about.

"This should be good," Angus said. He wore the smug smile a gamer gets when the final boss's hit bar is down to one last tick. Given that Angus was the biggest, meanest guy in the room, I knew the others would go along with him.

"But if it's some kind of stupid joke, you'll die even sooner," he added. "You wouldn't want that, would you?"

"No," I said. "I definitely don't want to die sooner."

I waited a second, to make sure I had their attention. There was little time to waste, but I've been a joker all my life, and I knew a bit about holding a crowd. This was going to be a tough crowd to hold, so I had to make sure I started off the right way. If I lost them before I even started, I was doomed. As soon as I was sure they were listening, I plunged into the story.

That was the key to keeping their attention—make it into a story. Our brains are wired to like stories. And I had an amazing tale to tell.

"I thought I'd found a genie," I said, diving right into the part they might find hardest to believe. I didn't waste time with the background details about uncovering an old brass bottle when I was digging in the yard, or even describing the bottle. Nobody cares about that stuff. And I didn't waste time explaining I was in the backyard because I'd gotten in a fight with my sister. That's where I go when I'm angry. Her boyfriend had given her a box of these awesome chocolates, and she wouldn't even let me have one. She just sat there, eating them, licking her fingers, and going, "Yummmm," right in my face.

I raced to the next part about my discovery. "But he was some other kind of magical creature who was far more dangerous. Genies grant wishes. This thing offered me a bargain."

They were all listening. Or, at least, all still looking at me. I knew the best way to keep their attention. I told the rest of my story like I was reading it out loud from a book.

"Anything you want," he said. "For a price."

"Chocolate," I said. "I want the most delicious chocolate ever made."

He rubbed his hands together, pulled them apart, and held out a piece of chocolate.

"What do I have to do for it?" I asked.

"Nothing, yet," he said.

I took it. I ate it. It was amazing. I can't even describe how great it was. I'd never tasted chocolate that wonderful.

"Want more?" he asked me.

"Yeah. I'd love more," I said. My mouth watered at the thought.

"You can have a whole box. A special box that will last a month, no matter how much you take from it. It will never become empty. But you need to give me something in return," he said.

"What?" I asked.

"Something special. What do you have to offer?"

"I can tell you a great joke," I said. "I know tons of jokes."

"That won't work," he said. *"I don't laugh at jokes."*

I wondered whether he was kidding, but he seemed dead serious. As I tried to think of something else, he said, "I have an offer. It should be easy for you."

"What?" I asked.

"You have to make someone laugh each day before noon, for a whole month," he said.

"No problem."

"But if you fail, even once . . ."

"You'll take back the rest of the chocolate?" I guessed.

He shook his head. "If you fail, you will die. Your death will be slow and painful. And that will give me pleasure."

"I was shocked," I told my stone-faced audience. "I'll admit it. I didn't want to risk my life. But these were *awesome* chocolates. And I knew I could do it. I make people laugh all the time. I'm a natural-born joker. And I managed to do it easily enough each day, especially since I had lunch at 11:40, and my friends like my jokes. Weekends weren't a problem, since I had plenty of friends who lived on my street."

Angus, who'd been leaning forward in his seat, started to lean back. I knew I had to get to the finish before I lost my battle against his limited attention span.

"But here I am. Stuck with you, and you aren't going to laugh at anything I say because, let's face it, you hate me. I'm the kind of kid you crush for fun. But I'm begging you, just this once, listen to a joke and let yourself laugh. I really do know some great jokes. And it feels good to laugh."

That was it. The moment of truth was here. My life was in their hands. I looked at each of them, one by one, and tried to guess what sort of audience I was facing. Did they totally not care about other people? Their eyes gave me no clue.

The clock ticked. I looked over at it. So did all of them. The two hands pointed straight up. They'd reached twelve, noon.

I gasped, clutched my chest, and fell to the floor. As I closed my eyes, I heard Angus laugh.

"Dead," he said. "Cool."

It was a nasty, mean-spirited laugh. But it was a laugh. And I'd made it happen.

"Get off the floor!" Mr. Spalter yelled as he walked back into the classroom clutching a large mug of coffee. He had no idea how perfect his timing was.

"Sure," I said, springing up. I was happy to be alive, and totally thrilled that I'd finished my month of making people laugh. Timing really is the secret to comedy, and to many other things in life. I had actually, as Angus threatened, died sooner. Though not for real. I knew the clock in this room was thirty seconds fast, like all the other clocks in the building. I'd checked that very carefully after I'd made the bargain. And I knew that at least one of the kids in the room would laugh at my death. That's the nature of bullies. Death and suffering amuse them. That's why I'd pretended to die when the clock in the classroom struck noon. And that's how I made someone laugh before my real deadline.

I slipped my hand in my pocket and grabbed a chocolate. A few minutes later, when Mr. Spalter was distracted with yelling at Angus, I popped it into my mouth.

It was delicious. It was worth it. But it was my last one. The month was over. The box would be empty when I got home. That wouldn't do. I guess it was time to hunt down that genie, or whatever he was, and ask for another deal. No joke.

GORDIE'S GONNA GIT YA

I guess a lot of kids would hate the idea of leaving the city where they were born. Not me. I couldn't wait to move away. However bad my new school would be, it wouldn't be worse than the one I'd left. I didn't have a single friend.

"Make friends," Mom told me at the start of each year.

She never explained how.

"Man up," Dad said.

Whatever that means.

At least we'd moved during the summer, so I wouldn't have to show up at my new school in the middle of the year. But, eventually, it was time for school, and time for me to meet my classmates and discover what sort of torments they might have in store for the new kid. The bus stopped right in front of my house. They had to do that, here. The houses are pretty far apart. I can't even see the next house from the road. Our new place used to be a farm. Mom and Dad bought it because they could run their business anywhere, and the city was an expensive place to live.

Here goes, I thought when the bus pulled up. I got ready for stares and sneers, and hoped I could find an empty seat.

"Hey, you're new," a kid said. He was sitting by the window in the second row. He was big, almost scary big, with short dark hair, wearing a T-shirt for a band I'd stopped listening to at least a year ago, and a ball cap with the logo of a tractor company.

"Obviously," I said. I waited for the first insult.

He patted the empty spot next to him. "Have a seat."

I looked down the aisle. There were some empty seats in the back.

"Come on," the kid said. "Before you get Orland yelling at you."

I guess Orland was the bus driver. I dropped into the seat. "Thanks."

He held out his hand. "I'm Leo."

A handshake? Seriously? "Duncan," I said.

We shook. His grip was way stronger than mine, but he didn't crush my hand. And he didn't mock me. He just talked about the things kids could do for fun in town, and asked me about where I'd come from.

Leo was on the football team. No big surprise, there. He was the quarterback. Again, no surprise. But he wasn't stuck up, like the star athletes at my old school.

That was a nice surprise.

When we got to the school, he introduced me to his friends. They all wanted to know about the city. Most of them had never been there. This was great.

Somehow, Leo even managed to get me onto the football team. It was sort of nice. I sat with the other players at lunch, and hung out with them after practice.

It wasn't until October that I first started hearing about Gordie. It was usually just one kid pushing another and saying, "Gordie's gonna git ya!"

The other would push back, of course, and say, "Nope. He's gonna git *you!*"

"Who's Gordie?" I asked Leo.

"Nobody," Leo said. "Kids just scare each other with stories about him. He's not real."

For someone who wasn't real, he sure got mentioned a lot. Eventually, I pieced a bit more of it together. Gordie was supposed to appear on Halloween. But that's as much as I could find out. I wasn't worried. Stuff like that just isn't real.

Halloween was on a Friday, which meant we had a football game before we could go out for candy. It started out badly. Leo threw two interceptions. Even so, the other team wasn't able to take much advantage of that. All they managed was one field goal. So we were just down three to nothing. And then, near the end of the fourth quarter, Leo called a play where I had to run the ball. It went perfectly. The whole team blocked for me. I got the ball into the end zone for a touchdown.

We won. I was the hero.

Everyone went wild. And then, they all slipped off while I was changing. By the time I got out of the locker room, the whole school felt empty. Now I was creeped out. But instead of going home, I went to the library. I wasn't sure what I was looking for, but if Gordie had some sort of connection to the school, the library was the best place to dig for information.

The school published a literary magazine every year, full of stories and poems, as well as drawings and articles. I found a stack of old issues and thumbed through the indexes.

And there it was, an article from six years ago, "The Legend of Gordie."

According to the article, fifty or sixty years ago, there was a kid nobody liked. His name was Gordie Vetnari. He didn't have any friends. Everybody picked on him. One night, on Halloween, some of the kids in town chased after him to steal his candy. When he was running away, he stepped right in front of a car. He got killed.

Every year since then, on Halloween, Gordie comes back to school and drags off the most popular kid, kicking and screaming. That kid is never seen again.

"Stupid story," I said. I got up from the table, leaving the magazine where it was, and stepped out of the library. I didn't get far. Someone was standing at the end of the hall.

"Must be nice to have friends," he said.

He was wearing a Halloween costume—cowboy hat and boots, gun belt with a toy gun in a holster, and a leather vest over a flannel shirt—but his body looked kind of funny, like it had been crumpled and then straightened out. And the hat was tilted at an odd angle.

"Who are you?" I asked.

Instead of answering, he said, "I thought it would be Leo. But you really snatched the title from him at the last minute. Nice touchdown." He stepped closer. Beneath the tilted hat, half his head was crushed. "Congratulations, Mister Popularity. You're my new best friend. For as long as you live. Which won't be long."

"No!" I screamed as Gordie grabbed my arm. "Leo's popular. He's the one everybody worships."

Gordie started to drag me down the hall.

"Think about it!" I screamed. "He's so popular, he could

46

make a total loser like me seem popular. He's making a fool out of you, just like they all did."

I didn't think it would work. But Gordie paused and stared at me with his lifeless eyes.

"Really," I said. "Look at me. I'm a jerk. A loser. Nobody would pay a moment's attention to me without Leo making it happen. He's way more popular than anyone in the school. Think about all he has going for him. Quarterback. Good looking. Charming. Strong. Nobody in the school is more popular."

"Yeah." Gordie dropped my arm. "Leo. You're right. He's the one."

He slipped off, leaving me trembling and gasping for breath. I was drenched with sweat and shivering at the same time. But I was alive.

Which is more than I can say for Leo. Sadly, he vanished that night. And when I say *sadly*, I really do mean it, because, with Leo gone, and with everyone remembering me as his best pal, and a sports hero, I'm going to have to work extra hard next year to make sure I'm not too popular when Halloween rolls around and Gordie comes back.

Look for me if you transfer here. I'm sure we can be great friends.

FAIRYLAND

t's a fairy circle!" Edwina shrieked.

"It is! It is!" her twin sister, Sadie, said.

They stood at the edge of the ring of mushrooms that Edwina had spotted in a far corner of their backyard. The dew-speckled fungi glistened, as if winking at the twins with a thousand joy-filled impish eyes.

"It can take us to fairyland!" they both said, in that unnerving simultaneous harmonized response that demonstrated why they'd never been placed in the same classroom. Or, at least, not for long.

The twins, who were deeply steeped in fairy lore, because everyone needs to be steeped in something, knew exactly what to do. They stepped inside the circle, being careful not to damage any of the mushrooms in the slightest. They faced each other and held hands. They chanted. (Chanting, of course, being one of the few times outside of a choir performance or a pledge when voices are supposed to ring out simultaneously.)

"Mother Mab, queen of the fairies, we beg you to allow us to visit your realm."

Nothing happened.

They tried again.

Still nothing.

Edwina dropped Sadie's hands. "You must have said it wrong."

"I said it perfectly," Sadie said. "You must have messed it up, somehow."

They tossed another round of accusations at each other. And another. Their eyes narrowed. Their faces reddened. Their fists clenched. They glared at each other and hurled the nastiest, most vile, and insulting names they could think of at each other. Simultaneously, they spewed identical words that would have made their parents gasp.

That did the trick.

They fell through the circle and landed elsewhere.

"It worked!" they both yelled, exchanging grins and hugs, since they never really meant those horrible nasty words. Everything was forgiven, of course.

They were in a meadow, at the edge of a forest.

The light was dim, as if the sun was just about to set.

The air was warm. The breeze was gentle as it wafted past and stroked their cheeks. It carried the scent of rotting garbage and sewer gas.

"What's that smell?" Edwina asked. She reflexively glanced over her shoulder, down toward her rear, as if she could have unknowingly been the source of the foul stench.

Sadie didn't answer immediately. She was busy throwing up. Edwina's stomach, in a display of twin empathy, decided that this was the proper response to the odor that assaulted them, and proceeded to spew its own portion of half-digested cereal onto the ground.

"I don't know," Sadie finally managed to say. "Whatever it is, it's dreadful."

"Oh, that's fairy dust," someone said, from behind them.

The twins spun, and found themselves facing a boy who looked to be about their age, though he was taller, and had pointed ears.

"I'm Pipsnip," he said, throwing the twins a wave and a grin. "Welcome to Fairyland."

"Does it always smell like this?" Sadie asked. She wiped her mouth with her sleeve.

Pipsnip sniffed the air, then frowned as if analyzing the results. "Not at all," he said.

"Well, that's a relief," Edwina said.

"This is pretty mild," Pipsnip said. "It gets a lot worse if the breeze dies down. But you'll get used to it."

"Where is everyone?" Sadie asked.

"In Glitter Castle," Pipsnip said. He raced off toward the trees, yelling over his shoulder, "Come on. Follow me." His feet seemed to dance above the ground, as if he were almost flying.

The twins, clamping their hands over their noses in a futile attempt to filter out some of the stench, followed Pipsnip through woods that seemed to be made entirely of dead or dying trees, strangled in dead or dying moss, tottering above dead or dying bushes.

Far in the lead, Pipsnip called back to them, "Don't touch the red ivy. It will burn your skin right off. And watch out for daffits."

The ivy was easy to recognize. It was red. Though not a very pleasant shade of red. The nature of daffits remained a mystery for a minute or two, until an enormous insect, the size of a pigeon, with a beak the looked like a hypodermic needle for vaccinating elephants, dived at Edwina. She swatted at it out of instinct. It burst on contact with her hand, showering her with something that might have smelled even worse than fairy dust. She didn't throw up. But only because her stomach was already empty. Sadie prodigiously managed to spew a bit more thin gruel from the depths of her digestive system, though she barely slowed her pace as she vomited, causing Edwina to dodge and dart in an effort to avoid the spray.

Soon, but not soon enough for the twins, they reached a clearing, where Glitter Castle sprawled before them like an enormous heap of driftwood jammed together by a giant who lacked any sense of design. As Sadie and Edwina got closer, they discovered the larger gaps between the pieces of wood had been caulked with what appeared to be animal dung. And not from a healthy, grass-grazing animal. Whatever animal had contributed its waste matter to the building efforts appeared to have a fondness for grazing on garbage or carrion.

"This can't get any worse," Sadie said.

It did.

Though sheltered from the foul wind, the castle lacked windows, or any advanced form of plumbing. It was mostly one large room, strewn with mats where the fairies slept and low tables where they ate boiled-daffit stew. Various animals wandered through the room, including several unicorns with broken horns and matted fur. Sadie reached out to pet one, but it hissed at her and snapped its teeth.

"That's it," she said, grabbing her sister's hand. "Come on, Edwina. We're leaving."

They stormed from the castle and ran back to the fairy

ring. It wasn't there. "Maybe this is the wrong place," Sadie said.

"It can't be wrong." Edwina pointed to the ground, which was generously splattered with the twins' first reaction to Fairyland. Large worms had showed up to dine at the edges of the regurgitated cereal.

"I guess it didn't travel here with us," Sadie said.

"Then how do we get back?" Edwina asked. "There must be a way."

Once again, Pipsnip spoke from behind them. "Give it some thought, you brainless ninnies," he said.

The girls spun toward him, too startled to be offended by his words. In truth, brainless ninnies often fail to catch the meaning of unpleasant things hurled at them.

"It's obvious," Pipsnip said.

The breeze, which had blown softly ever since they'd arrived, finally died down. As the air grew still and heavy, the true stench of Fairyland hit Edwina so hard, she could barely speak. "What's obvious?"

Unable to join the chorus at the moment, since she was too busy choking on the stench to speak, Sadie shook her head and spread her hands, as if hoping to be handed the answer.

Pipsnip stared at them with a mix of anger and sorrow. "Do you think, if there were a way out of this horrid land, anybody would stay here?" he asked.

The twins stared back, silent.

"We've been searching for an exit for centuries," Pipsnip said. "There isn't one."

Edwina's and Sadies's jaws dropped in dismay, but only briefly. They snapped their mouths shut as the awful taste that accompanied the true stench settled on their tongues. They quickly learned to keep those mouths shut as much as possible, which did make Fairyland a teeny tiny itsy bit more pleasant for everyone. At least, until summer ended, giving way to the slippery rains and flesh-eating tadpoles of slime season.

And they lived miserably, in stench, filth, and squalor, ever after.

OFF THE BEATEN TRACK

My brother doesn't talk much. Actually, Joey doesn't talk at all. But he's good with math. He carries this old calculator around with him. It's the kind with a big screen that can do graphs. He's always playing with it. It's not random. He isn't just stabbing his fingers at the buttons. I can tell that much, even though math isn't my best subject. I'm pretty sure Joey got all the math genes in our family. Don't ever think, just because he doesn't talk, that he's stupid or anything. He understands me. He's really smart. I can tell.

He also loves trains. He has tons of train books in his room. We go to the ridge to watch the passenger train roll by, on its way from Richford to Delta Falls. There are two trains a day. One each way. The westbound train has to slow down a lot before it reaches the trestle, because there's a sharp curve ahead of the approach. So there's plenty of time to see it before it picks up speed.

During the school year, we can only catch the 7:00 PM eastbound run, after dinner. In the summer, we can go out for the 11:55 AM westbound run, too. We don't go out every day, but it calms Joey to watch the trains, so I try to take him as often as possible. Sometimes, we'll climb the slope all the way down to the trestle, so we can feel the trains rumble by. There's a lot of power in all that steel. But we never go on the trestle. Everyone around here knows not to do that. It's a single track. Go on there when a train is coming, and you've got two choices: jump eighty feet into a shallow river full of large rocks, or get hit by a train. I think it's probably the same choice either way. A slow train packs as much punch as a long fall.

We were on the ridge when the creepy guy showed up. The train had already come by, at 11:55, looking as awesome as always, but I felt like sitting there for a while, soaking up the nice weather. And Joey had his calculator, so he was happy. If I stayed right there for ten hours, he'd be good.

I didn't hear the guy coming. I guess I was lost in my thoughts. But I felt it when he plunked down next to me. And I heard the crunch of gravel, and the clack of small stones rolling down the slope. He was an adult. Long-sleeved shirt. It looked expensive. New jeans. Hiking boots. But not the kind for serious hiking. They were the kind you bought to make people think you hiked. It was hard to tell how tall he was, seated there, but he seemed pretty solid.

I looked at him, figuring he'd say something. But he just stared back. His eyes gave me the shivers. It was creepy enough he sat right down next to us. The silence made it even worse. I glanced over at Joey, who was punching buttons and paying no attention to the man.

"Let's go." I got up. So did Joey. He was used to doing what I asked, as long as it was what he wanted to do.

The guy stood, too. "Sorry," he said.

"What?" I asked.

He reached toward his belt right behind his hip and pulled out a hunting knife. Sunlight flashed off the blade. It looked like it had just been cleaned and polished.

"Sorry it's you. It has to be someone. I've been waiting. Watching. Looking. You come a lot. Patterns make it easy."

This can't be real, I thought. But it was. I was in the woods near the train tracks, facing a killer with a knife. My only chance was to run. Trying to escape uphill would be a mistake. It was a steep climb. I was good at scrabbling, but Joey was slow. We had to run on the tracks.

Which way?

The tracks away from the trestle cut through an even steeper valley, with no easy path back up for at least three miles. We'd be trapped. We had to run across the trestle. It was about a half mile, but that would get us to the road. And to houses. We'd scream. People would come help us.

It would be safe to go on the trestle. The train had already crossed. There wouldn't be another one until evening. And Joey would follow me. We just had to stay ahead of the guy for a short stretch.

"Who's first?" the guy asked. He pointed the knife back and forth between Joey and me, as if playing a choosing game.

"You!" I shouted. I gave him a hard shove. He didn't fall. But he staggered back.

"Run!" I screamed at Joey. I grabbed his arm and yanked him toward the tracks. He ran. I ran. The guy ran.

The guy was big and angry. We were small and scared. But we were faster. And we had on sneakers that were meant for running. We'd put five or ten yards between us and him by the time we got to the middle of the trestle. I could hear him panting. We were going to make it.

"Keep running," I told Joey, risking a lungful of air I hoped I wouldn't need later.

We were three quarters of the way across the trestle when I heard the whistle.

No mistake. I knew what it was.

Freight train!

They almost never come along. Maybe once a month. But one was coming now. I could see smoke in the distance, moving in a curving path above the hills as the train followed the tracks.

I froze for an instant. Then I looked over my shoulder. The guy froze, too. But not for long. He turned and ran back the way we'd come. I guess he needed to live more than he needed to kill. At least, at this moment.

That didn't make things any better for us. Following the guy meant death, delayed. I knew he'd be there, waiting, and kill us as soon as we got off the tracks. I looked down, and felt my stomach squeeze into a tight ball of fear. Death lay that way, too. Not just for me. For Joey. He was older, but it was my job to protect him. I'd always done that. I protected him from cars when we crossed the street, and from bullies when we were in town.

We had to follow the killer. There was no other choice. A tiny chance to survive was better than no chance at all. Maybe I could tackle him really hard and send us both over the edge. At least that would save my brother.

I turned back that way. "Come on, Joey."

"No!"

If I wasn't already frozen, I would have been nailed in place by that shout. My whole life, I'd never heard Joey say a single word.

"We gotta run, Joey," I said. "We have to get off the tracks." Maybe he was more scared of the guy with the knife than he was of the train. I guess that made sense. He loved trains. He probably couldn't imagine that something he loved could hurt him.

Joey waved the calculator in my face. I waited for him to say more, but instead, he ran toward the train.

"Come back," I shouted.

He did. But only to grab me and start dragging me with one hand while waving the calculator with the other. If I fought back against him, we'd die right there.

I stopped struggling and followed him, running toward the train that would flatten us beneath tons of steel, or knock us into the gorge. Even if the engineer saw us, there was no way he'd be able to stop in time. I could see the front of the train, now, as it cleared the curve and entered the approach to the trestle. I could hear the engine strain as it started to pick up speed.

We ran. I looked back. The guy was heading toward safety. He looked back, too. I guess he wanted to see us die, even if he couldn't kill us himself.

I followed Joey, running toward the train that was barreling toward us.

It turned out to be a brilliant idea. We reached the end of the trestle, and dived off the tracks onto solid ground, just seconds before the train shot past.

As we lay there, sprawled on the ground, Joey tapped the calculator again. There was nothing on the display. But that's when I understood what he was trying to say.

Trust me. I know math. I know trains.

I thought about those algebra problems where a train is

going somewhere and you have to figure out when it will arrive. That's what this was. And the answer was tricky. We were closer to the side of the trestle where the train was coming. Joey had figured out, somehow, that we needed to run that way to get off in time. I moved up the ridge a bit and I looked toward the other end, just in time to see what would have happened to us if we'd run away from the train.

It didn't feel good watching the killer get killed by the train. It didn't feel good at all. But it felt right.

"You saved us, Joey," I said.

He didn't say anything. He never said another word, the rest of our lives. But I know he understood me. And I understood him a little better, too. That's how it is with brothers who look after each other. I might not be great with math, but I know that sometimes one plus one is a whole lot more than two.

THE SWORD IN THE STEW

And there appeared in the land of Caerleon an enormous pot of stew, half the height of a full-grown knight, filled to the bubbling brim with an assortment of savory meats and flavorful vegetables. As if the sudden appearance of a meal fit for a king wasn't wondrous enough, a gleaming sword protruded from the center of the stew, its hilt studded with sapphires and rubies, its point buried deep in the bubbling broth. And, as if even a sword fit for a king thrust into a meal fit for a king wasn't wondrous enough, a gleaming message meant for an aspiring king was carved deep into the surface of the pot, encircling it right beneath the rim:

He who removes the sword from the stew shall be the rightful king of Caerleon.

Caerleon, it should be pointed out, was at that time without a king, due to a prolonged and unfortunate battle among the heirs of the previous king, Althberthinkle the Bloody Handed, who had recently died a peaceful death after waging a long lifetime of wars, battles, sieges, forays, assaults, and skirmishes. He'd also left behind thirteen sons, and no clear instructions about his wishes. By all accounts, Althberthinkle wrongly believed he'd live forever.

Those peasants who first passed by the pot after its miraculous appearance stared in wonder at the sight, but could not read the writing, and thus had no idea why there was a sword in the stew. The cooper, curious about the sword, grabbed it by the hilt and gave a yank. The sword remained firmly in place.

"Step aside, weakling," the blacksmith said. "No barrel maker can match my strength." He grabbed the sword with two sinewy hands, placed a boot on the edge of the pot (causing the baker, who had wandered up to the fringes of the crowd, to flinch in horror at the proximity of mud and meat), and yanked with all his might.

The sword budged not a hair.

An educated merchant who was passing through the town, selling elixirs to cure all ailments, maladies, and illnesses, read the inscription aloud. Word spread quickly after that, and soon reached the ears of those who felt capable of ruling the land and deserving of the crown.

Sir Langly, the oldest of the potential heirs to the throne, arrived first. "Make way!" he shouted at the growing mob that pressed toward the stew. "Let the rightful king of Caerleon prove to all that he is worthy to rule."

Given that he emphasized his words with a broad wave of his own sword, the crowd was quick to obey. Sir Langly sheathed his sword, grasped the hilt of the sword in the stew, and gave a mighty tug.

The sword moved not at all.

In a short time, the remaining heirs arrived, and also failed. Knights from across the realm traveled to Caerleon, hoping to claim the crown. Princes from other lands came in droves, yearning for their own kingdoms. Kings and caliphs, hoping to expand their rule, arrived in quantities greater than a trickle but less than a stream. Tsars and khans came, along with emirs and oligarchs. They all failed to pull the sword from the stew.

"Make way," a gentle voice called, after the last of the princes, kings, and caliphs had given up. A man cloaked in robes, his face concealed within the folds of a draped hood, approached the edge of the crowd. He made his way to the front, and stopped within reach of the sword. All who watched, from cooper to blacksmith to heir, laughed at the robed man. He raised both arms, but did not reach for the hilt. Instead, in a louder but still gentle voice, he called, "Have at it, lads and lasses."

A mob of little beggars, the castoff orphans who roamed the streets in search of scraps of food or discarded objects with any remaining value, surged toward the pot in the wake of the hooded figure. They, the sons and daughters of the many victims of wars, waved crude spoons recently carved from fallen wood.

As they devoured the stew, it quickly dropped below the rim of the cauldron. Meat and carrots, potatoes and turnips, simmering in a rich gravy, all fed hungry mouths eager for a warm meal. Each new sliver of the blade that was revealed gleamed, showing all who looked that it was too pure and mighty to be soiled. No bit of stew clung to it.

Soon, the pot was half-empty. Still, the orphans feasted. The instant each one ate his fill, he'd step away and another would take his place. In moments, only a quarter of the pot remained. The hooded man moved his hand within reach, but still made no attempt to grab the hilt.

The feasters dwindled, until only four remained. Two left, followed by the third. The stew was nearly gone. All but the far tip of the sword was now revealed. When the last lass to fill her belly scraped away the final piece of meat, resting against the tip of the blade, the sword tilted, falling into the waiting hand of the hooded man.

He grabbed the sword and raised it with one hand, pushing back his hood with the other to reveal his face.

Um, not *his*, actually.

Hers.

"The baker's daughter!" the blacksmith cried.

It was, indeed, Samara, the daughter of the baker. She was known to sneak scraps of food to the orphans, and find warm clothing for them as each winter approached.

"A woman!" someone shouted.

"She can't be king," the blacksmith yelled, waving his hammer.

"No woman can rule," three of the heirs cried, each unsheathing his sword.

"This sword says otherwise," Samara told them, still speaking softly. With a flick of her wrist, she swung the sword, slicing through the thick oak shaft of the blacksmith's hammer and cutting the three heirs' swords neatly in half.

There were no other arguments.

And so Samara became king of Caerleon. Or queen. She cared not what she was called. And though she had won the throne by way of the sword, she ruled the land with peace and mercy. And stew. Lots of stew for everyone.

THE DOLL COLLECTOR

Can I please go** with you?" Pamela asked as her mom dragged her by the arm toward Great Aunt Hester's front door.

"No," her mom said. She held onto Pamela with one hand while she pressed the doorbell with the other.

"Pleeeeeaassse?"

"I've already explained this a dozen times. I have business meetings on the road all week. I check into a crummy little motel each night, get up each morning, eat a crummy breakfast, drive to the next meeting, and then drive to the next crummy motel. There's no way you can come. Now just settle down. It's only five days."

"It's a crummy five days," Pamela said, echoing her mother's favorite description for unpleasant things. "And it's six, counting today." Six days, five nights—however she counted her time away from home, Pamela felt it was unbearably long.

The door opened a slit, letting out a column of air that smelled of mildew and menthol medicated creams. Great

Aunt Hester peered out through the crack, stooped so low she seemed to be hunting for something she'd dropped on the floor.

"Why Pamela! What a delight. Come in. I'm making pudding." She turned away, shuffled several steps, then turned back and said, "It's butterscotch! I make it from scratch."

As the crack widened from a slit to a passage, Pamela stepped into her great aunt's house. For a moment, the dank smell and gloomy air kept her from noticing the worst part. But as her eyes adjusted to the half darkness, she realized she was being watched. Eyes aimed at her from all over. Eyes, and in some cases, empty holes where eyes had been. Pamela shivered like she'd just plunged through thin ice into freezing lake water.

"What the . . . ?" Too startled to finish the sentence, she raised a hand and pointed at the shelf that ran along one wall of the living room, a foot and a half from the ceiling. The other three walls held similar shelves.

"Oh, those are my babies," Great Aunt Hester said. "You'll meet them later. Come on. Let's get you some pudding."

Pamela tried to tear her eyes away from the shelf. But it was like turning away from someone you knew was staring right at you. As she followed her great aunt through the house, she saw there were similar shelves on nearly every wall in every room. Dozens of shelves. All holding doll heads. Nothing else. No stuffed animals or porcelain birds. No ceramic mugs or painted plates. Just doll heads. No bodies. No arms or legs. Endless doll heads. Some had hair. Some were bald. Some were tiny. Some were larger than life. Some were perfect. Others were cracked or chipped. Some lacked eyes. All were creepy.

Pamela turned back to her mom and mouthed the word *Please*.

Her mother responded with a silent *No*.

In the kitchen, a vat of light brown glop bubbled on the range. It looked like mud mixed with the yellow goo that comes from crushed insects.

"Ready for pudding?" Great Aunt Hester asked.

"Maybe later," Pamela said, fighting against the need to gag. "It was a long trip." All she wanted to do was lie in bed, close her eyes, and pretend she was somewhere else.

"Of course. What was I thinking. Let's get you settled. You must be tired after that long trip." Great Aunt Hester led Pamela down the hall to a stairway, and then up the stairs to the third floor. They went down another hall, which ended with a closed door. A hand-lettered sign written in purple marker and taped to the center of the top door panel read: "Welcome Pamela!!!!!"

"I know you'll have a great time," Pamela's mother said, giving her a hug.

As Pamela slipped free of the embrace, Great Aunt Hester turned the knob and gave the door a push. "I'll let you settle in."

"Thank you."

Pamela took a deep breath of the heavy air and faced the room.

Please, no, she thought as she stepped through the doorway.

But it wasn't "no." It was "yes." Sixteen times. Sixteen shelves. Four on each wall. Doll heads all around the room. Old, creepy doll heads with wide open eyes that stared at her. And it seemed as if all the ugliest and creepiest heads had been saved for this room.

Pamela looked past her great aunt, to her mother, ready to make one last plea for rescue. But her mother was already heading back downstairs. Pamela wanted to race after her, but Great Aunt Hester still blocked the door.

"I'll let you unpack," she said. "Come down when you're finished and we'll have a nice chat."

Pamela unpacked as quickly as she could. She knew that fleeing from this room wouldn't get her away from the constant presence of doll heads, but it would spare her from being alone with them.

She went downstairs, and enjoyed an evening that was exactly as mind-numbingly boring and dreadful as she'd feared. But her fear of bedtime was even greater, so she sat there and listened while Great Aunt Hester told her the name of each head, along with its history. The pudding did not help. Apparently, Great Aunt Hester didn't think sugar was an essential ingredient.

Finally, after watching her great aunt doze and wake several times in a living room chair, Pamela realized she had no option except to go to sleep, herself.

After saying good night, she headed up the stairs. "It's just dolls," she said. "Not even whole ones."

The pep talk did little to calm her down.

She tried not to look up at the shelves as she got ready for bed. Instead, she studied the meager furnishings. The bed was narrow. There was a floor lamp next to it, plugged into an outlet in the corner, behind a dusty upholstered chair that didn't look very comfortable. Across the room from the bed was a dresser with six tiny drawers, where she'd managed to cram most of her clothes.

Just once, her gaze slipped, and locked on a large, hairless baby head, with pink cheeks, huge blue eyes, curled lashes, and puckered lips, sitting on the top shelf above the bed.

"Ugly!" Pamela said as she tore her eyes away from the head.

Pamela climbed into bed, pulled up the covers, and tried to ignore the feeling that she was the target of hundreds of unwelcoming eyes. She reached for the lamp switch and turned off the light. As she settled her head onto the over-stuffed pillow, the slightest sound tickled at her ears, like someone was lightly shaking a bag of marbles. She sat up and turned on the lamp.

The sound died. She waited a minute, then killed the light and tried once more to go to sleep.

Again, the tiny clicks and clacks taunted her.

She listened carefully. The sound seemed to be coming from right above her head. She sat up, moving as quietly as possible, then reached for the lamp's switch. But she didn't turn the light on, yet. First, she closed her eyes, so she wouldn't be temporarily blinded. Then she switched on the light and opened her eyes, looking in the direction of the sound.

There it was! One of the doll heads, the pink-cheeked one she'd stared at before, was shaking, as if trying to escape the shelves. Driven by equal surges of anger and horror, Pamela stood up on the bed, grabbed the head by the cheeks, and shouted, "Stop it!"

The head responded by clamping its mouth down on her palm.

Anger and horror became horror and pain. Pamela flung her arm out in a reflex action. The head slammed against the opposite wall, bounced to the floor, and started rolling back, its mouth opening and closing with sharp clacks.

Acting totally on instinct, Pamela leaped from the bed and

landed hard on the head with one foot. She felt a frightening and satisfying crunch as her heel destroyed the wretched thing.

"Take that," she whispered.

The thrill of victory was rapidly replaced with the certainty that she'd badly cut her foot on the sharp edges of the broken pieces. She lifted her foot and saw she'd escaped with just minor cuts. The same couldn't be said about her victim. The head was shattered. One eye, loose in the middle of the debris, blinked. Pamela let out a yip of surprise, and jumped back. She waited, but nothing else moved.

She's going to kill me, Pamela thought. She looked around the room. There wasn't even a waste basket. She grabbed a T-shirt from the dresser, spread it out on the floor, and gathered the crushed pieces. She saved the eye for last, reluctant to touch it. Finally, she flicked it with one finger so it rolled onto the shirt.

She folded the shirt and stuck it in her suitcase. That got rid of half the evidence. She waited, to see if any of the other heads would move. They didn't. But there was a large gap on the shelf that her great aunt would instantly notice in the morning.

"I can fix that," she said. She stood on the bed and cautiously placed the tip of one finger against a pair of lifeless lips. This head didn't try to bite her. Still, each time she touched one of the heads as she spaced them out to erase the gap, she expected it to open its mouth and scream at her. But nothing bad happened.

At least, nothing bad happened while she was awake. Her dream, on the other hand, was not pleasant. She was on an endless street, running from a doll head as big as a boulder. It rolled after her, trying to crush her. Every time she looked over her shoulder, it was closer.

She stumbled and fell. The head reached her, but didn't keep rolling. Instead, the mouth opened, engulfed her, and crunched down.

CHOMP!

The sound shot through the room. Caught in the transition from dream to reality, Pamela wasn't sure, at first, what had awakened her. But in the echoed memory of the sound, she knew it wasn't part of her dream. She lay there, listening to the silence of the room, for what seemed like hours before falling asleep.

She slept poorly, woke early, and drifted through the next day, hoping the sun would never set. Before she got in bed that night, she looked at the doll heads and said, "Leave me alone."

This time, the CHOMP that woke her was followed by a second chomp. She heard it clearly. It was not a dream. All the heads on every shelf had opened their mouths and then clamped down, like snapping turtles, biting so hard they rocked a bit and rattled against each other.

On the third night, there were four chomps. Once again, the first one woke her. "Stop!" she screamed as the heads snapped their jaws and rattled on the shelves.

Halfway through the eight chomps of the fourth night, Pamela jammed her palms over her ears, closed her eyes shut, and screamed a wordless cry of terror.

"Last night," she said, the next evening. She scanned the shelves. The heads stared back, inanimate. She saw no sign of life. It would be over, soon. The heads would scare her one more time, and then she'd be free of them.

When the first chomp woke her, she forced back her scream and started counting. If the pattern held, there'd be sixteen chomps. She could survive that.

The first head fell on the third chomp, hitting her on the shoulder before it bounced to the floor.

"Ouch!" Pamela touched her shoulder. A sharp pain told her she'd been bitten.

Three more heads fell on the fourth chomp. And then, another dozen on the fifth, raining down on Pamela, and on the floor from all sides of the bedroom. As Pamela rolled out of bed, she realized each chomp, starting with the single one on the first night, had moved the heads slightly forward on the shelves, pushing them toward the edge, and toward their chance for vengeance.

Now, they were all falling. Pamela lost track of the count. A large head smacked her on her own head, staggering her. Others bit at her heels as she stumbled away from the bed.

"I'm sorry," she screamed. "It was an accident. I didn't mean to do it."

The apology fell on unhearing ears. In her desperate rush for the door, Pamela stepped on one of the heads.

Her ankle twisted.

She fell face forward toward a carpet of chomping heads.

She tried to catch her fall with her hands, but the doll heads beneath them rolled away. Her hands slipped out. She fell flat, right onto dozens of doll heads.

"Stop . . ." It was a whimper, now.

The heads swarmed over her, still chomping.

"No . . ." It was a whisper.

Mercifully, Pamela's intense fear masked most of the pain as the doll heads chomped away at her body, head, and limbs. Eventually, she felt nothing at all.

And then the room fell silent. And all the dolls closed their eyes.

PHYSICS FOR TOONS

I **was hanging out** on Saturday morning with my pal Drury. He had this awesome TV that covered half a wall, and some sort of enormous satellite dish on the roof that got a zillion channels.

"Nothings on," Drury said after flipping through the whole lineup twice.

"Let me see." I reached for the remote, which was about half the size of a small book. I wasn't surprised he'd failed. He zips through way too fast. "I'll find something."

Drury held the remote out. Right before I could grab it, he pulled his hand back and punched me in the stomach with his other hand.

"Sucker!"

"Ouch. Cut it out."

He was always doing stuff like that. But that was okay. I always got him back.

He held out the remote again. I raised my right hand shoulder high, like I was about to swear an oath, or offer to answer a question I wasn't sure about, and wriggled my fingers to get his attention. When I saw my fingers had caught his eye, I snatched the remote with my left hand. He reached for it, but I punched him in the ribs with my right and stepped out of range.

"Even?" I asked.

"Even," he said as he rubbed his side.

I flicked around for a while, slow enough to actually see what was on each channel, but fast enough that I'd have a chance to get through all of them before morning turned into afternoon. I finally found a channel that was showing a cool cartoon.

"What's this?" I asked.

"Never seen it before," he said.

Me, either. It had a couple cats, the sort who look like cats but walk on two legs like people. They were chasing some mice around. The usual stuff. But it was really violent. That was a plus.

There was plenty of dynamite, giant boulders, chain saws, and vats of acid. The cats and mice seemed to suffer about equally, which I felt was really fair of the people who made the show. At one point, when a cat flattened a mouse under a steam roller, Drury shouted, "Radical!" and slugged me in the shoulder.

I went flying.

Really.

The punch lifted me right off my butt. I flew into the wall, making the whole house shake, then bounced across the room to the opposite wall, and came down on my head.

When I sat up, little chirping bluebirds flew around my head in a circle. On the screen, the steamrolled mouse inflated himself back to normal by sticking his thumb in his mouth and blowing on it. (Yeah, he had thumbs. Hey, if a cat can drive, a mouse can have thumbs.) The mouse ran off, hopped into a tank, and opened fire on the bulldozer. Around my head, the birds turned into stars.

"Whoa, you okay?" Drury asked.

I nodded. I was fine. It hadn't hurt at all. It had actually felt sort of fun, like a carnival ride that flung you around real fast. I stood up, swung my arm back behind me, and then I swung it forward in a big circle. "Got you back!" I shouted as I thumped Drury on top of his head with my fist, which had grown to the size of a large ham during the windup.

He squished almost flat, then sprung up, making a noise like an accordion. He went up and down a couple times, but finally ended up back the way he'd been before I'd slammed him.

"Awesome," he said.

We both looked at the screen, where a mouse was shooting a cannon at one of the cats. The cannon ball went right through him. The cat bent down, looked at the hole in his belly, and shook himself hard, like a wet dog. The hole disappeared. I checked my fist. It was back to normal.

Drury turned toward me. I turned toward him. We both grinned. "It's like we're in our own cartoon," he said.

I answered him, but kept my voice low. When he leaned closer to hear what I was saying, I grabbed his hair and yanked. He shot off his feet. I spun around, holding onto his hair. He whipped around me, faster and faster. Finally, I let go, sending him feet-first into a wall.

He crashed into it, rocking the house. His body flattened. Then he slid down to the floor like a human pancake. He stuck his thumb in his mouth, and blew himself back up, just like the mouse had done. I started to wind up for another smack-down punch. Drury dashed at me, grabbing a book as he ran past the couch. Before I could squash him, he swung the book hard, hitting the side of my head like it was a baseball. My head shot off my body and bounced around the room. That was the weirdest, coolest thing I'd ever felt.

I watched my body walk toward my head, staggering with my arms out, until I stumbled across it. When I bent down to pick it up, Drury dived for it like he was trying to recover a fumble.

If he wanted to play football, I'd be happy to help out. I nailed him in the chest with a kick, like I was aiming for a forty-yard field goal. Try doing that when your head is on the floor looking up at your body. I connected perfectly.

Drury shot up, smashing into the ceiling. The whole house bounced up and down, this time. As I stuck my head back on, I tried to figure out what I could do to him next.

That's when I heard a creak, followed by the shriek of ripping wood. I guess Drury had hit the ceiling so hard, he'd knocked the satellite dish loose. I saw it crash to the ground in the front yard.

The TV went black. The box beneath it flashed a message: No signal.

No signal meant no more cartoon. And no more cartoon physics, I guess. Because Drury fell straight down, hitting the carpet with a sound they don't use in cartoons. After which, he said a word they definitely don't use in cartoons.

Drury moaned. I stepped over to see if he needed help. At least, that's what I tried to do. Everything was so wrong, it took me a moment to even begin to understand what had happened. I could see the large number 37 on my shirt. That number was on the back of my shirt. Just the back. Not the front. That meant either my shirt was on backwards or . . .

As my brain leaped from puzzled to panicked, I reached up with both hands to touch my face. All I felt was hair.

"Your head is on backwards," Drury said, echoing my realization.

I turned around so I could face him. Even though I knew I had to put him behind me in order to see him, it felt hugely wrong to move that way.

Drury started laughing.

"What's so funny?" I asked.

He pointed at me and shouted, "About face!"

"That's not funny," I said.

"Sure it is," he said. "You're just looking at it the wrong way." He paused, as if it took him a second to realize the full meaning of his words. Then he cracked up again.

I backed toward the door.

"Make sure to look both ways when you cross the street," Drury said.

I left the house and stumbled my way down the stairs.

Behind me, Drury called out, "Don't worry. I won't talk behind your back."

As I reached the sidewalk, a thought hit me. If that was how my best friend acted, I really wasn't looking forward to how everyone else treated me.

Looking forward . . .

Great. Even I was doing it to myself. I tried to push those thoughts from my mind as I headed home.

Headed . . .

Wonderful. I hoped his parents would get the satellite dish fixed. And I hoped I could find that cartoon again. If not, I'd be spending the rest of my life seeing where I'd already been.

THE HEART OF A DRAGON

To live forever, one must capture the heart of a dragon.
—An old saying of the village

Only five of us escaped the village when the dragon attacked. It was a small male. I could tell that from his size and color. Though even a small dragon is huge and fearsome. Most of the younger men and women ran toward the dragon, bravely trying to defeat him. They failed. Most of the elderly and all of the children ran into the woods to the north. But other creatures in league with the dragon awaited them. The ground grew red with slaughter, and the air grew heavy with screams as the fierce and hungry creatures pounced. I'd also raced for the woods, but I saw the carnage in time to swerve aside, follow the tree line, and head for the grain fields to the east. So, as I soon learned, did four others.

We escaped the village.

But we did not escape the dragon.

He herded us, moving through the air with a swiftness that

seemed impossible for a creature that size. We ran, in blind terror, straight into the pit he had dug for us. It wasn't a deep pit, but it was lined with netting. Before we could scramble out, the dragon seized the edges of the netting and lifted us into the sky, like we were a rich harvest of wriggling fish plucked from the river.

We tried to untangle our limbs. It was difficult, at first. The jostle of powerful wing flaps shook us as the dragon gained height. Then, he leveled off, gliding across the sky, and our passage became smoother. As I pushed myself to a free area of the netting, I took note of who was with me. Three boys: Emeric, Asher, and Destrian. And one other girl, Marissa. We were all born the same year, and old enough now to help with chores but not yet old enough to be put in charge of anything.

Marissa was crying. So were Asher and Destrian. Only Emeric seemed to be showing any spine.

"We have to escape," I said.

He reached for the knife at his belt. "I could cut the net."

I looked down, and felt a new stab of fear join the terror that was already surging through my body. "I'd rather not escape capture by falling to my death," I said. A spine and a brain rarely grow in the same body.

"Falling?" Marissa forced the word past her sobs.

"Quiet," I said. "Go back to weeping. We don't need your interruptions."

I kicked Asher to get his attention. "Do you have any thoughts?"

He shook his head.

Destrian had his eyes closed tight. I kicked at him, too, but that just made him turn away and whimper.

We failed to find a plan.

The dragon brought us to his aerie, on the flattened top of a mountain. And then he flew off, leaving us to wriggle free of the net and explore our prison. Or, perhaps, our tomb.

"Too steep," Emeric said, kneeling so he could peer over the edge without danger of falling.

"Goats can climb this," Destrian said. He wiped at his runny nose with the back of his hand. "Maybe we can, too."

"Then give it a try," Emeric said. He gave Destrian a slight push, though not enough to move him far. Still, Destrian let out a yelp.

I stepped away from them and went to see how Marissa was faring. She'd curled into a ball, arms clutching her knees. I wanted to tell her something comforting. But nothing I could think of would serve that purpose.

I moved past her, toward one of the treasure piles scattered across the mountain top. At least we wouldn't starve. Assuming we lived long enough for that to happen. The dragon had looted all manner of things. There were sacks of grain, bundles of dried meat, and other provisions. Past that, a depression on the surface of a large rock held rainwater. So we wouldn't suffer thirst, either.

"What do we know about dragons?" Emeric said.

He was addressing all of us.

"They're immortal," Marissa said.

We'd all heard the old sayings. Some said dragons were immortal. Others said dragons could grant immortality to those who had captured the dragon's heart. Yet others claimed an elixir of immortality could be made from that very same heart, if it was pulled while still beating from the chest of a living dragon. They did not say how to accomplish this without being burned all the way down to the bone.

"What do we know that might *help* us," Emeric said. "And might be true."

"They're sly and treacherous," I said. That was easy to see. Our captor had led us into a trap he'd set. That took more than natural animal cunning. That took thought and planning. Even many people weren't capable of that.

"This one might want to keep us alive," Asher said, kicking at a bag of grain. "That's not dragon food."

"But why?" Emeric asked.

The answer seemed simple. And horrifying. "To fatten us up," I said.

Marissa let out a sound somewhere between a howl and a whimper. I shuddered, myself, at the idea that I was now livestock.

No!

I wouldn't accept that. I was not born to be a dragon's meal.

The dragon returned, but paid no attention to us. The same couldn't be said for us. We paid a lot of attention to it, hoping to discover anything that might help us escape, or give us a clue to our fate.

Dragons, we soon learned, lived much of their lives in stillness. Our captor would lie on his belly, with his head at the edge of the cliff, staring off. Not moving. Not blinking.

As the hours of our captivity became days, we talked among ourselves, but we had no idea what to do, or what the dragon planned to do to us.

On the fifth day, he flew off again. When he returned, I saw blood seeping from his shoulder, just above the wing joint. That gave me an idea. But I didn't want to share it, or any benefit it brought me, so I waited for the others to fall asleep.

Among the sacks of treasures and provisions, there were

several bags stuffed with roots and herbs. I recognized most of the plants, and knew their properties. I took valderspawn, mixed it with comsprey, added a few drops of water, and crushed it into a paste between two rocks. Then I approached the dragon, walking toward his injured side.

"This will heal your wound," I said.

He regarded me with an intelligent eye.

"Do you understand?"

The head moved slowly up and down. I took that for a nod.

Then, the head turned toward me and the mouth moved. I braced for a crackling wave of fire, but instead heard a rumbling sound. No. Not a sound. I realized it was words.

"Yes. I understand."

So he could speak.

I rubbed the salve on the wound and sang the healing song, keeping my voice low so it wouldn't carry to the others. The dragon seemed to sigh, but said nothing more.

As I returned to the bed I'd made from cloth sacks and the pelts of sheep, I realized I finally had a plan, though not necessarily one of escape. It was more about survival. I would win the dragon's heart. Whatever it took, however long I had to work toward my goal, I'd win his heart for my own. I had everything I needed, here, on this mountaintop, and nothing left for me back at what remained of the village. I looked at the others, who slept nearby. It would be vital not to let them know what I intended, lest one of them try to best my efforts and win the dragon's heart in my place. Marissa would do that, for sure. As might Emeric.

So I tended the dragon and cared for him in every way I could. I sang to him, softly, when the others slept, and baked treats for him in the crude oven we had constructed, hiding them among the loaves I made for our own meals. Nobody seemed to mind that I did all the baking.

One night, as I was waiting for the others to fall asleep, Emeric crept up to me, moving with the silence of a thief or assassin. "Ssssshhh," he said, placing his hand over my mouth. "I have something to show you."

I got up and followed him across the flat ground as he roused the others. When we'd all gathered behind a treasure pile, out of view of the dragon, Emeric lifted a deer skin and revealed three swords and two pikes.

"I've been searching quietly, all this time. I finally found a weapon for each of us." He pointed toward the dragon. "He sleeps. If we all rush at him and attack the head, we can kill him. He might be powerful, but so is a thrust through the eye into the brain."

"And then what?" Destrian asked.

"There is cloth. Plenty of cloth," Emeric said. "We can make a rope long enough to reach a spot where the slope is less steep. And then, we can climb safely to the bottom."

"We can't kill a dragon," Marissa said.

"We have to try. We have no other choice," Emeric said. "Who is ready to fight for our freedom?"

He stared at us, one by one. Each of us nodded, including me.

"The eyes," he said as he handed us our weapons. "Strike hard, straight, and true. Strike deep with a pike on each side. Strike the neck with swords, or plunge the point toward the heart, if you can."

We crept across the ground, three on one side of the sleeping dragon, and two on the other. Emeric raised his pike high above one eye, Asher raised his above the other. Destrian and

Marissa readied their swords in trembling hands. I remained near the center of the dragon's body, close to the heart. Not to strike, but to avoid a strike.

"Wake up!" I screamed as I threw down my sword hard, letting it strike the stones at my feet like a warning bell.

The dragon woke. In a move too swift for me to follow, he struck Emeric with his head, flinging him high in the air and off the mountain top. The scream took a long time to fade. By then, the others had followed him in his fate, flung to their deaths.

I stood, panting, Marissa's last pitiful wail ringing in my ears. I would miss her least of all. That thought made me smile. As did the image of the dragon seizing her head and shoulders in his jaws before flinging her far off.

"I'm sorry," the dragon said.

"Don't be. They mean nothing to me." Though this was true, I was startled by the coldness in my voice. And I was puzzled by his apology. "We had no need of them."

"I am immortal," the dragon said, rising.

I was surprised he told me that without being asked. "What is your secret?" I knew he'd share it with me. And I'd live forever. Here, with him, it would be a perfect life. Anyone could capture the heart of a duke or a prince. Who else could say she'd tamed a dragon, and won his heart?

"This is our secret." He moved closer, and lowered his head so it was a whisker's width away from mine.

"Tell me," I said. I'd bake a special cake for him, tonight.

"We are born with the weakest of hearts," he said. "We are pathetic creatures."

He raised a front limb and raked one claw down his chest, opening himself like he was slicing a ripe fruit.

"Many of us do not even live long enough to see the end of our first year. We are sad little worms. But there is a way to grow strong. A way, even, to live forever."

I clenched my fists, eager for the next words, hardly believing I was about to learn the deepest of all secrets.

He put a claw behind me and pulled me forward to his gaping chest. I saw something small and shriveled inside, quivering with a barely visible beat. My hands dropped to my sides.

"We can take the heart of another," he said. He raised the other claw and punctured me just below my throat. "But for the heart to be strong enough, for the heart to last more than a few years, it must be filled with love."

He slit me open and pulled me against himself. I felt my heart push through the gap in my chest, as if eager to find a stronger home.

"Thank you, my love," the dragon said.

As my pain gave way to darkness and my screams gave way to silence, I gave my heart to the dragon.

SEARCHING FOR A FART OF GOLD

'm not in the mood for this," Julian said. He nodded to the left. We were sitting on my front steps, catching our breath after an attempt to replicate the highlights of the Mixed Martial Arts bout we'd watched last night.

"Oh, great." I shuddered when I saw Kenny Siznik heading toward us. He was the grossest kid I knew. Sometimes, the stuff he did was funny, like when he used his nose as a pea shooter. Other times, he was just disgusting. He was always spiting, sniffing, scratching, burping, or farting.

I pointed over my shoulder at the door to my house. "Should we go in?"

"Too late," Julian said. "He already spotted us. We don't want to get on his bad side."

"Good point." I shuddered again when I thought about what Kenny had done to Danny Rabin's sandwich last month when Danny wasn't looking. I was pretty sure it would be years before I could look at chicken salad again without feeling the urge to throw up. No way I wanted Kenny for an enemy. It was bad enough being someone he liked.

"Hey, guys. Wuzzup?" Kenny said when he reached us.

I shrugged. "Nothing."

He opened his mouth to say something else, but then he got a funny look in his eyes. "Uh oh—breakfast is kicking in." He spun away and bent over, pointing his butt right at us.

To make things even worse, his pants were so low, his butt pretty much popped out. I rolled off the stairs as Kenny let out an enormous fart. The air seemed to ripple. Luckily, I managed to avoid the line of fire. Or line of fart, I guess.

Unfortunately for Julian, he wasn't fast enough to escape like I did. I looked up to see him getting blasted.

"You idiot!" he screamed at Kenny, who was laughing so hard, he dropped to his knees.

"Sorry," Kenny said as he stood back up. "I think it was the turkey sausage I had with my pancakes. It's a new brand. Farmer Browning's Gooble Gobblers. Super tasty. Oh, man, that really was a stinker. Good thing we're outside." He waved at the air in front of his nose and grinned. "Mom buys them because they're supposed to be full of healthy stuff, but I'm pretty sure there's something in them that turns from solid sausage to gut gas the instant it reaches my intestines."

He plopped down on the steps, like we were the best of friends. We had to put up with him for half an hour before he got bored and wandered off. At least he didn't fart again.

"He makes me sick," Julian said.

"Me, too. Hey, what's that?" I pointed to his shirt, where something glistened against the dark blue material just to the right of the Steelers logo.

"Oh, no," Julian said after he'd glanced down. "It's stained."

There was a shiny patch on the front of his T-shirt, the size, and roughly the shape, of my thumb. But it didn't look like a stain. Stains don't glitter in the sunlight. It looked sort of hard. I reached out and tapped it, half afraid that, despite the shine, it would turn out to be mushy or sticky.

Clink. It was neither of those things.

"It sounds like metal," I said.

"It can't be." Julian touched the blotch, first with the tip of one finger, and then with his whole hand. "You're right. It's metal. That's weird."

"It could be gold," I said. "I mean, it's gold colored, and it's metal."

We stared at each other. Then we looked over toward Kenny's house. "You think it was the fart?" Julian asked.

"It had to be." I pictured the way Julian had been blasted. "I'm pretty sure the gold wasn't there before Kenny came over. I would have noticed it."

"Gold . . . ," Julian said. "That would be awesome." He managed to peel the metal off his shirt. It was about an eighth of an inch thick.

"Let's get it tested," I said.

"How?" Julian asked.

"There's a place in the mall that buys gold. They have that big sign: *WE BUY GOLD*. They'll know if it's real."

Julian and I headed across town. The gold place was actually one of those little shops in the middle of the floor, like the coffee cart and the piercing stand.

"Will you buy this?" I asked the guy behind the counter. He had short black hair and a thin mustache, neither of which stood out as much as his bright green blazer and gold bow tie.

I was afraid he wouldn't take gold from a kid, but he didn't seem to care who was on the other side of the transaction.

He looked at the gold, weighed it, then said, "Not very high quality."

"You're not a very good liar," I said. I'd watched him. He'd hidden his amazement pretty quickly, but I knew he'd been impressed by something.

"Okay," the guy said. "It's not exactly the lowest quality."

"There are plenty of other places where we can sell this," I said.

"You got me, kid. It's high quality. I can give you eighty bucks for it. Believe me, that's a fair price."

"Eighty!"

Julian and I both shouted the word. The guy put the gold into a large lockbox, and counted out four twenty-dollar bills.

"Thanks," I said.

"Come again," he said.

"Oh, we will."

As we walked off, I handed half the money to Julian. "Fifty-fifty split?"

"Sure."

That's the kind of friend he is.

"Why'd you say we'd be back?" Julian asked.

"Because this is too good to quit," I said. "It's easy money, and lots of it. We need to get more gold."

"Which means we have to get Kenny to eat a whole lot of that new sausage," Julian said.

"That shouldn't be hard." I smiled at the image of Julian and me pushing turkey sausages into a funnel shoved down Kenny's throat. "But how do we get him to fart on you again?"

Julian looked like he was going to gag. "Maybe there's a better way. Let's kick around some ideas."

So we kicked around the problem. I'm not even sure which

of us shouted out, "Camping trip!" first. But it was a great idea. We'd invite Kenny to go camping with us. We'd cook up a ton of those sausages for dinner. He'd fart all night in his sleep. (We'd learned the hard way, two years ago, how much Kenny farts in his sleep, thanks to the one and only time until now he'd been part of a sleepover.) The next morning, when we got into our swim suits to go to the lake, one of us would hang back and get the gold from his pajamas.

Kenny was thrilled when we told him about the trip. It was the perfect plan, except, as we discovered to our horror that night, Kenny didn't sleep in pajamas, anymore. Now, he slept in his underwear.

As we expected, he farted in his sleep all night. Way before midnight, as the air inside grew from foul to deadly, Julian and I fled the tent. We dragged our sleeping bags outside, to sleep under the stars. Still, every time I heard another blast of gas fleeing Kenny's intestines and trumpeting its way past his butt cheeks, my brain added in the sound of the crinkle you get when you clutch a stack of twenty-dollar bills.

By morning, I guess Kenny was nearly farted out.

"Last one in the lake is a loser!" he screamed, rushing out of his tent.

That's not the best way to wake up. It's even worse when it's accompanied by a rear view of Kenny running down the trail, his underwear sagging in the back like it was carrying a big load. The tiny remaining farts he released as he ran toward the water made it sound like he was being chased down the path by a flock of ducklings.

"There goes our gold," Julian said as he wormed himself free of his sleeping bag.

"We'd better follow him," I said as I unzipped my bag.

We got to the lake just in time to see Kenny let out a whoop and do a cannonball off the dock.

There was a huge splash at the impact spot.

And then, nothing.

Julian and I ran to the edge of the dock. "He's trapped!" I said.

Kenny was four feet down, in a seated position, anchored to the bottom of the lake by the weight of the gold in his underwear. He was thrashing his arms, trying to swim up. His lips were clamped shut, but his eyes were wide open. He was looking wildly around. I realized he had no idea why he couldn't get to the surface.

"He's going to drown," I said.

"Maybe not," Julian said.

"What do you mean?"

"I think he's sinking under the silt on the bottom. So he might suffocate, instead."

Julian was right. Kenny was starting to sink beneath the lake bed, dragged down by the gold in his underwear. Not that suffocating would be any better than drowning. "This is awful!"

"You have to save him," Julian said.

"Me? No way." I definitely didn't want to swim under that water and pull off Kenny's underwear. Especially if I had to feel for it under the silt. "You do it."

"Are you kidding? This was your idea."

"Our idea."

"Mostly yours."

"Mostly ours."

Kenny, who was now halfway buried, opened his mouth to yell for help. I guess he'd spotted us. Screaming would be a very bad idea. There was no time to argue. I dived into the water. So did Julian. We really did make a great team. We swam down and yanked off Kenny's underwear. It wasn't easy. He fought us all the way. I guess he was panicking. But we did it. And once the deadly weight was removed, we managed to get him out of the water and back onto the dock before he drowned.

I looked down at the lake bottom, trying to spot the underwear. There was no sign of it. Maybe we could try to recover it, later. But it was probably still sinking, dropping far out of reach. Right now, I just wanted to get into dry clothes and forget the past minute of my life forever.

"Got any more of those sausages?" Kenny asked as we walked back to our tent.

"No!" Julian and I shouted.

Sometimes, the price of gold is just too high.

ON ONE CONDITION

I've got my little brother to the point where his right index finger never leaves his nose. It's funny and disgusting at the same time, which is always a good combination. My older sister scratches her head pretty much nonstop. That's also pretty funny.

It didn't take long to make those things happen, either. Brothers and sisters are easy. My parents were going to be harder. Dad's at work most of the time. Mom only has a part-time job, so she's usually here when I get home from school, but she doesn't really listen to what I say. She just snatches the key words out of the sound stream—stuff like "broke," "smashed," "failed," and things along those lines. I haven't really tried it with them, yet.

But Toby, my little brother, was ridiculously easy. It started when I was surfing the channels and came across a program about the history of science. I'd heard about the series, because I knew my teacher liked it. But I'd never checked it out until now, because *history* and *science* were not subjects I normally associate with entertainment. They were showing this dog. I stopped to see what the episode was about, because I love dogs. They explained how the dog would start to drool when it knew it was going to be fed. So, for a while, they'd ring a bell, and then feed the dog. Eventually, the bell, all by itself, would make the dog drool, even before the food came, and even if the food didn't come.

I sort of understood that. Donny Wackworth used to punch me in the shoulder every time I walked past him. After a while, just seeing him coming my way made me flinch like I'd been punched.

The show got more interesting than just talking about drooling dogs. The thing that happened with the dogs was called *conditioning*. But there were two kinds. The kind with the bell was called *stimulus-response conditioning*. The bell was the stimulus. The drooling was the response. In the same way, Donny's fist was the stimulus, and my flinch was the response.

But there was another kind of conditioning, where you do something good or bad after the behavior, to reward or punish it, instead of before. It's like, if every time you pick up your socks from the floor, you get a small shock, you'll learn to stop picking up your socks pretty quickly. But it works the other way, too. Imagine if, every time you picked up your socks, you heard your favorite song. Or if, every time you scratched your chin, someone gave you a dime. After a while, you'd be picking up socks or scratching your chin all the time. You might not even be aware you were doing it.

I didn't have unlimited dimes. But I had something else that Toby ate up. He was hungry for praise. Every time he had his finger anywhere near his nose, I praised him. Like if he was doing a drawing, I'd say, "Toby—that's an awesome drawing." If his finger was actually in his nose, I praised him even more.

It worked. I couldn't believe it at first. It seemed more like sorcery than science. But I had definitely controlled his behavior. Then, I tried conditioning my sister. She was dying for nice words, too, so it was just as easy with her as it was with Toby. I guess I could have had her do all sorts of weird things, like standing on one leg, but head scratching seemed pretty funny, so I went with that.

There was no way I could keep quiet about this forever, once I saw how well it worked. I needed to brag. I wanted someone to know how clever I was. I decided I'd tell Ricky Morales. He's not a close friend, but he sits next to me in class, and we like lots of the same stuff. I got to school right before the bell rang. Our teacher, Mr. Skinner, was up front, ready to take attendance. We're supposed to sit quietly when we're in the room, but I couldn't wait. I had to tell Ricky about the way I controlled my brother and sister.

"Guess what?" I said to him.

"What?" he asked.

"I came up with the coolest—"

"You all look so smart and well-groomed and ready to learn," Mr. Skinner said. "You are the best students I've ever had."

I clamped my hand over my mouth. So did Ricky. So did all of us.

"You are such a marvelous class," Mr. Skinner said. "You're the best I've ever had."

I kept my hand there all day. I'm not sure why. I just couldn't move my hand away. And Mr. Skinner kept telling us how wonderful we were. He's a really great teacher.

I still wanted to talk to Ricky about conditioning and how I totally ruled my little brother and sister. I knew he'd be impressed by my ability to control other people. But I guess that would just have to wait until class was over.

GHOST DANCER

I'm a nerd and proud of it. I love math and science. I want to make amazing discoveries and do brave things when I grow up, like my heroes, Marie Curie, Ada Lovelace, and Grace Hopper. I want to explore superconductivity or invent a better battery. I want to discover a new type of laser. I want to become the world's leading expert in stealth technology or seismic prediction. I want to change the world and improve the lives of people and animals.

But right now, sitting on a chair in the gym in Alexander Fleming Middle School, all I want is to reach the end of the Spring Dance. I don't even know why they call it a dance. It should be called a *sit*. Or a *snack*. They play music. One or two kids actually dance. I don't really care whether I dance or not. I'm just as happy observing people. Most of the other girls want to dance. But a lot of them come from really old-fashioned homes, and they've been taught they have to wait to be asked. My friend Deborah's folks are so strict, they won't let her wear shorts to school. And Molly's mom won't let her go to sleepovers. It's like we're stuck fifty or a hundred years in the past.

I think the boys want to dance, too. But they're too shy to ask. Or too scared about getting rejected in front of their friends. That's a shame. I know Deborah would love for Jayden Simmons to ask her.

As I said, I don't really care, either way. Whether any boy wants to dance with me or not doesn't change who I am or affect my worth as a person. They don't get to define me. But I also know there's nothing wrong with wanting to be asked to dance. I hope Deborah gets her wish. If she does, it will have to be soon. It's 7:40, and the dance ends at 8:00.

I've been checking my watch all evening. So have the boys. They're waiting for *her*. They've been whispering and looking over at the door of the girls' locker room pretty much constantly. According to the story, she always appears ten minutes before the end of the dance. Nobody knows who she is, for sure. The rumors are so old, my dad heard them when he was in school here. Most of the stories involve her dying on the way home from the dance. Though some say she died on the way there. There's even one version that claimed she died during the dance, when a fire broke out. But there's never been a fire in the building. I'm absolutely positive about this. It's pretty easy to research stuff like that.

Nobody even knows her name. They just call her *The Girl in Blue*. Not very imaginative, but pretty accurate. That's one thing all the versions agree on. She wears a blue dress.

"Wow, seven forty-five, already," I tell Molly, who is sitting to my right. Out of habit, I glance from my watch to the clock on the wall, and then back to my watch.

"Time for more punch," Molly says. Her folks don't let her drink anything with sugar at home, so she goes a bit wild whenever there's punch.

She dashes over to the snack table. But she bumps it, splashing a big wave of punch onto the floor.

"Poor Molly. I'll get some paper towels," Deborah says. She leaves her chair and heads for the hall.

I can't resist calling after her, "Watch out for the Girl in Blue."

I check how Molly is doing. She's grabbed some napkins. The teachers are helping her mop up. Just as they're about to finish getting everything cleaned, Molly stumbles again, spilling more punch. She's such a klutz.

I know, before I even look back at the locker room, that something has happened. The music plays on, but the world beneath it goes silent. And then, the world gasps. As I turn my head, my eyes sweep past the seated boys. They're all staring at the door to the girls' locker room, with their jaws slack and their lips gaping.

And there she is. The Girl in Blue. All blue, in a full-length dress with a very high collar. Half visible. You can see the locker room door behind her. She drifts toward the boys. Two of them hurdle the backs of their chairs and flee the gym. The rest remained seated. Some seem transfixed. Some elbow their friends and whisper, "Ask her." On either side of me, I can sense that the other girls are transfixed, too.

After several rounds of *ask her* and *no, you ask her*, one boy stands and walks over to the Girl in Blue. Jayden. I figured he'd be the one. For some reason, boys who are irrational enough to be afraid of girls aren't rational enough to be afraid of ghosts.

Jayden stops a few feet from the Girl in Blue, and speaks. His voice is too quiet to reach my ears. But it must have reached hers. She nods. They step toward each other. They dance for a magical and timeless span of time. The song ends. As Jayden drops his hands from her back and shoulder, she leans forward and gives him a kiss on the cheek. That's absolutely forbidden at dances, but a quick check reveals the teachers are still occupied with the spill.

The kiss breaks the spell that had gripped the onlookers. The boys whoop and cheer. Jayden returns to his peers, a hero who wasn't afraid to approach a ghost. The Girl in Blue glides to the locker room and slips behind the door.

A moment later, Deborah returns from the hallway. She has no paper towels, of course. That wasn't her mission. Her task was to dash to the other door to the locker room at the end of the hall, get the specially designed dress we'd stashed in her locker, and become a ghost. I glance toward the punch bowl, where the teachers are just finishing the cleanup. Molly reaches me at the same time as Deborah.

"How was it?" I ask.

"Nice." Deborah says. "I liked it. Thanks."

"It was my pleasure," I say.

"And thank you, Molly," Deborah says.

"Any time." Molly raises a paper cup of punch and says, "Here's to our genius friend, and her cloaking cloth."

I shrug off their praise. "It was no big deal. I just adapted some current technology."

I'd explained all of it to them right after I got the idea to take advantage of the urban legend about the Girl in Blue and help Deborah get what she wanted—a dance with Jayden. And I got to try out my invention. The fabric uses fiber optics to bend light, so the wearer appears to be transparent. It's far from perfect, which is actually perfect for anyone who wants to look like a ghost. I'm glad Deborah was brave enough to make an appearance as the Girl in Blue, and that Molly was willing to help distract the teachers. I wish Jayden knew who he'd danced with. But this was a good first step.

"Next dance, you're on your own," I say to Deborah.

"No problem," she says. "If I can find the courage to become a ghost, I can do anything."

"That's for sure," I say. And if I can create the illusion of a ghost, I can do anything, too. But I already knew that.

CHECK OUT THE
LIBRARY WEENIE**s**

Check out the library weenies," Brutus Thumpbuster snarled as he rumbled down the hallway past the open door of the Chelsea Middle School Media Center. I didn't look up from my book. I knew his face, that snarl, and those mean-spirited, beady eyes all too well. I gripped the book cover tighter, eliciting a crackle of protest from the protective Mylar wrapper, and reminded myself that I was safe from harm in this media-walled sanctuary.

We all were—me, Diego, Rivka, Faber, Raj, Patrizia, and Meiying. There were others who came and went, but the seven of us pretty much always hung out in the Sofa Circle or sprawled on the scattered bean-bag chairs before school started. The Book Rats. That's what we called ourselves. It's okay to call yourself a rat. It's not okay for someone else to call you that. Or to call you a weenie.

After Brutus had moved along to his next target, I glanced at Ms. Denwilter. She would have said something to Brutus, if she'd heard him, but she was all the way back in the far corner of the room. She was busy pulling some old books from the shelves. I really liked her. She let us come here and read before the first bell. And every time I thought I'd read all the good books ever written, she'd suggest another author for me to explore. She was like a book magician. And she really cared about us. She called us her Diversity Crew. Not because we came from a lot of different cultures, but because we read all sorts of different things. I loved science fiction. Raj read *The Lord of the Rings* trilogy over and over. Rivka was big on technology and math. You get the idea.

When the first bell rang, I headed for home base, moving safely in a sea of students. I'm small for my age. Small for any age, I guess. Though I hope that the growth spurt Dad keeps promising I'll get shows up before I make my way through high school, college, the work force, and retirement. Until that spurt, I'd have to continue to spend a lot of my time trying to fly beneath the radar of bullies like Brutus.

It's funny the way people get names that fit them, almost like life is a book written by an author who wants to give you a hint about what's going to happen. Brutus seemed perfectly named. As for me, I got saddled with Timothy Meagher. Yeah, it's supposed to be pronounced *Mayer*, according to my parents, but you know it will inevitably become *Meager* in even semi-mean hands. Or mouths. And I've been called Tiny Tim more than once. Or *Timidthy*, which I at least have to admit is a bit clever. I guess it could be worse.

And that's exactly what things became when county inspectors discovered the library was infested with a dangerous form of mold—worse. They ordered the room to be sealed off. Nobody could go in, and no books could go out, until experts dealt with the problem.

I learned the news at the end of the day, when I swung by

the library to stock up on books for the weekend. There was yellow tape across the double doors, like the kind they use at crime scenes, and a big *CLOSED* sign on the wall for those who weren't literate in the language of tape. Ms. Denwilter was standing in the hallway, staring at the door, her head slumped, along with her shoulders.

"Closed?" I asked. It was not my most brilliant conversational moment, but I was too surprised to come up with anything more clever or supportive.

"Closed," she said. "Mold."

"Must have been those old Hardy Boy books," I said.

She didn't even smile at the joke. Not that it was all that funny. Mr. Denwilter had taken over as our school's media specialist in the middle of last year, when our old librarian, Mr. Yancey, won two million dollars in the state lottery and quit the next day. There were a ton of books he should have gotten rid of, including some series fiction that was getting dangerously close to the century mark, and several shelves full of reference books that seemed, based on their warped appearance, to have encountered a minor flood. But he hadn't been enthusiastic about making any changes. Ms. Denwilter had totally the opposite attitude, and she was making progress. But it was a big job.

On the way home, I wondered what I would do when I got to school on Monday morning, since my sanctuary was currently lethal. And I tried to figure out where I would get books since our town didn't have a public library.

"How was school?" Mom asked when I came in.

"Okay. Except the library is swarming with deadly mold."

"That's nice." She went back to the blog post she was writing. I went through my old books, looking for something good.

By Monday, I still hadn't figured out what to do. I caught up with Diego a block from the school. "We can't go to the library," I said.

He stared at me for a moment before responding. "You have a gift for stating the obvious."

Before I could reply, Rivka came running up to us. "Guys! You'll never guess what I found!" She spun around and headed back toward the school. "Come on! Everyone else is already there."

We followed her to the side of the school and around to the back, where she pointed to a small mountain of cardboard boxes that were currently being investigated by our fellow rats.

"Books!" I shouted when I saw what was stacked up and tumbling out of the boxes.

"Old, damaged books," Diego said. He'd gotten there ahead of me, and was already pawing through the contents. "I guess Ms. Denwilter finally got them out of the library."

"Just in time for us," I said, squatting next to Diego and checking the titles on the spines. "Hey, some of these look interesting."

As I was thumbing through an ancient book, I heard the last thing I'd ever want to hear.

"Check out the library weenies."

I turned and saw Brutus walking toward us. "Or are you garbage weenies?" he said. "Do you know what's going to happen to you?"

"This is trash," Diego said, ignoring the threat. "Not garbage. There's a difference. It's a common mistake, like with *soil* and *dirt*. You'd know that if you ever bothered to pick up a book."

Correcting a bully's grammar is also a mistake. Brutus let out a howl, clenched his fists, and charged at us.

We all ran for the nearest entrance. Outside, we'd be antelopes fleeing a lion. Inside, we had a chance to get lost in the crowd. I'm small, but I'm fast. Not as fast as Diego or Meiying, but I wasn't far behind them. Even Raj, in last place, had a respectable lead over Brutus. We hit the door hard, pushing it open, and scampered down the hallway as fast as we could.

"We're doomed," I said, once we'd blended in with our classmates. "We're safe for now, but he's going to be waiting for us after school."

"We need to figure out a strategy," Diego said.

"It's Monday," Meiying said. "We can meet during free period."

That was a great idea. We had a free period Monday, Wednesday, and Friday, thanks to a schedule nobody really understood. We usually met in the library.

"Where should we go?" Raj asked. "We can't hang out in the fortress of moldiness."

Faber pointed toward the end of the hallway. "How about the art room."

"Perfect," I said. The school had cancelled all the art and music classes because of budget problems. There was never anybody in the art room. After spending the morning peering over my shoulder to make sure Brutus wasn't about to pounce on me, I slipped along the corridors and gathered with the other Book Rats in the sad remains of the art room.

My friends twitched and shivered in various ways, like rats who were aware that doom was approaching. We all looked at each other with hopeful eyes, as if one of us could save the day. I finally broke the silence. "Brutus is right. We *are* library weenies."

"What's wrong with that?" Diego said. "The best way to fight against bad words is to embrace the insult, and take it for your own. I'm proud to be a reader. I'm proud to be a Book Rat. And I'm super proud to be a library weenie!" He thumped his chest.

"Me, too," I said. "But that doesn't mean I have to be a wimp. I want to stand up for myself."

Raj stood up straighter. "So do I." Then he slumped a bit. "But Brutus would crush me."

"So let's not try to fight brute strength with brute strength," Diego said.

Patrizia smirked. "You mean brute weakness, in our case."

"Either way," I said, "what's our strength?"

"Book strength!" Rivka shouted, raising a fist in the air.

"Right. We're readers," Diego said. "We think, and we know things."

"Knowledge is power!" Raj shouted.

"Yeah! There are tons of books where the little guy wins," I said. Naturally, I was a big fan of the little guy. "So what do we know about fighting evil?"

"We need a champion," Diego said.

"Batman!" Faber said.

"Or a dragon," Meiying said.

"A real champion," I said. "Let's embrace being library weenies. Every answer is in the library. Right?"

"Sure," Raj said. Then he shook his head. "But the library is closed, and we're not in it."

"We've read all the books," I said. "We're the Diversity Crew. Between us, I'll bet we've read every book in the library. This is like the world's biggest version of Battle of the Books. We're getting tested on everything we've ever read."

"I'm up for that!" Faber said.

I was starting to get excited. Maybe we really could save ourselves. "So, who are the heroes we know about," I asked.

"David slew Goliath with a sling," Patrizia said.

"Killing is frowned upon in schools," I said. "As are weapons. We don't need a weapon. We need a champion."

"Legolas!" Raj shouted, naming an elf from the *Lord of the Rings* books.

"We'd have better luck finding Gollum," Diego said.

I shuddered at the thought of that creepy creature, who was also from *Lord of the Rings*.

"Gollum!" Rivka clapped her hands. "That's it. You just gave me the perfect idea."

We all voiced variations of "Huh?" and stared at her.

She slapped a big block of clay that sat on the floor next to her. "We'll make a golem! This is the best idea ever."

This did not clarify things. I waited for an explanation.

"The golem is a clay monster that protected the people in the Jewish ghetto," she said. "There are dozens of versions of the story. In one, the golem is brought to life with an amulet containing the secret name of God."

"And you would happen to know this name?" I asked.

"No. But in the other version, he's animated with the word *emet*. That means *truth*."

She tore off the wrapper and scratched some Hebrew letters on the slab of clay. I could swear it seemed to quiver. Before I could really focus on it, she smeared the letters away. "Come on. If we all pitch in, we can make a clay figure before the period ends."

"But it's just a legend," Diego said.

"No. My grandfather told me that his great-grandfather had seen the golem," Rivka said. "It's real. I believe in his existence. Where I come from, we know there is truth behind our stories and traditions. I'm going to get started. It's up to all of you to decide if you want to help."

Well, I liked playing with clay. And even if this was not going to save us, it would at least give us something to do. Which was better than standing around wondering which bones of ours Brutus would break.

"How big does he have to be?" I asked.

"We want a giant!" Raj said.

"There isn't enough clay," Patrizia said. "And there isn't enough time."

"As big as Brutus," I said. "That should be enough. This golem, he's clay. He can't be hurt, right? He'll be magically strong. So he doesn't have to be a giant."

"He?" Rivka asked. "Why not *she?*"

"It doesn't matter," Patrizia said. "Let's go with *it.*"

So we made it—a creature of clay—using all the clay we could find, which was a lot, since the old art teacher was passionate about pottery. Our defender was far from perfect, and very far from pretty, but anyone with a bit of imagination would see it as having the form of a person. It was taller than I was. That's no surprise. It was actually slightly taller than all of us.

"We did it!" Rivka shouted.

"Library Weenies unite!" Raj yelled.

We echoed his cry.

"Now what?" I asked as I stepped back to admire our work.

Once again, we were interrupted by an unwanted screech.

"There you are!"

It was Brutus. I guess he'd heard our cheering. He rushed into the art room, kicking a table out of his way as he stormed toward us.

"This better work," I said as Rivka reached up and inscribed *emet* on the golem's forehead.

It worked.

Big time.

The clay hardened before our eyes, making a sound like truck tires on loose gravel. The golem rose, expanding so his head touched the ceiling.

"Defend us!" Rivka yelled, pointing at Brutus.

The golem grabbed her arm and threw her across the room. She slammed into the wall and dropped to the floor.

Before I could move, the golem grabbed me by the shirt in one giant clay fist and Raj by the other. It lifted us up and started shaking us like we were cans of soda it wanted to squirt in the faces of unsuspecting victims. Its own face lacked all emotion. I saw nothing but a clay mask with dead eyes and an unmoving mouth. I tried to pry its hand open so I could slip free, but beneath a thin layer of soft clay that squished against my fingers, I felt solid rock.

"What's happening?" Raj shouted.

Unfortunately, I knew the answer. "The monster is turning on his creators," I said. Our voices vibrated all over the place as the golem shook us.

"That's a classic mistake," Patrizia said as she yanked without success at the arm that held me. "We should have known. Didn't you ever read *Frankenstein?*"

"I sort of skimmed it," Julian said.

"Me, too," Diego admitted.

Across the room, Rivka sat up, but stayed where she was. She looked pretty stunned. I had more immediate things to worry about. The golem spread his arms wide, like he was planning to slam Raj and me together. It would definitely hurt to become part of a pair of human cymbals.

Past the golem, I saw Brutus shake himself out of his startled state. But he didn't run away from the monster. He ran toward us. Great. Now we were under attack by two monsters.

"It's no use," I shouted at my friends. "Save yourselves."

Brutus leaped up and swiped at the golem's forehead. I had no idea why he was attacking it, but I knew the blow wouldn't have any effect.

The golem froze. He was no longer shaking me. I was still shaking, but that was my own nerves doing the work.

"What . . . ?" I asked.

"How . . . ?" Raj asked.

"Huh . . . ?" Rivka said as she rose slowly from the floor.

"Don't you library weenies know anything?" Brutus asked. He sounded the way my folks did when I'd done something brainless.

"Apparently not." I pried at the golem's fingers, but they were still locked solidly in place.

"You give the golem life by writing *emet*," Brutus said. "You stop it by erasing the first letter." He pointed at the forehead, where *emet* had become *met*.

"Death," Rivka said. She stared at Brutus. "I didn't know that part of the story. And I didn't know you were Jewish."

"I'm not," Brutus said. "I know about Odin, and I'm not Norse. I know about Osiris, and I'm not Egyptian. I know about Cu Chulainn, and I'm not Welsh."

"Me, too," Rivka said. "Good point."

"Thanks for saving us," Raj said.

Brutus shrugged, as if his heroic actions against a deadly clay monster hadn't been a big deal.

"Yeah, thanks. I thought I was doomed," I said. But there was something I needed to know. "Why are you mean to us?"

"Why do you stare at me like I'm a monster?" he asked back. "And why did you make fun of me when I was trying to warn you not to touch the moldy books? Did you want to get a respiratory infection?"

It looked like the golem wasn't the first monster I'd foolishly helped create. I felt a flush of embarrassment in my cheeks as I ran some of our past encounters through my mind and saw them in a new light. I didn't have a good answer. Maybe we had started the whole problem somehow, long ago, by making assumptions about him.

I changed the subject. "You like to read?"

"Doesn't everybody?" Brutus asked. "Hey, I saw one of those little free libraries right down the road. You know—the box where you can get a book or leave one for someone else. There's still time before the bell rings. We can sneak out through the window. Who wants to go grab a book?"

Everyone chimed in affirmatively. And they slipped out, racing each other to be the first to reach the library.

Still dangling, I looked over at Raj. "It could have been worse."

He nodded. "Agreed."

We managed to slip out of our shirts and drop to the floor. Then we extracted our shirts from the golem's lifeless grip.

"Looks like there will be one more library weenie," Raj said as we headed out to meet up with everyone and get something to read.

"I'll let you be the first to call Brutus that," I said.

But when he did, Brutus smiled, because it's good to be a library weenie, and it's perfectly fine to be kidded by one of your own.

CALL ME

My parents finally got me a phone. It's not a real fancy one, but it does everything a phone should do. I can download apps, play games, and text my friends. I don't think I'll use it much to call people. Nobody does that, except my parents. But just for fun, after I'd set everything up, and figured out how to find my own number, I called myself. As I tapped the icon to connect, I wondered whether I'd get to leave a message on my own voicemail. That would be sort of fun, and sort of geeky.

Instead of an electronic greeting, I heard, "Hello?" It was a kid's voice. I didn't recognize it as one of my friends, but it sounded sort of familiar.

"Hello," I said back, too surprised to say anything else.

"Who's this?" he asked.

"Who's *this*?" I felt like I'd been zapped back to first grade, where the height of cleverness often lay in repetition.

"You called me," he said.

"I called *me*," I said. "I was calling my own number."

"So you must have gotten you," he said.

We both fell into silence for a while as we let that sink in. Now I understood why the voice was so familiar—I'd been hearing it all my life.

"You're me?" I asked.

"So it seems," he said.

"Lance?"

"Yup."

"Lance Kirkenwald?"

"The one and only," he said. He pretty much instantly followed this with, "Or so I thought."

"Where are you?" I asked. I pictured my other self floating in a cloud somewhere.

"In my room," he said. "Sitting on the corner of my bed, staring at the clothes I was supposed to fold."

"Me, too," I said. "Now what?"

"We hang up and forget this ever happened?"

"I'm not sure I can forget this," I said.

"Me, either."

There was another long gap. I guess I really didn't have much to say to myself. It's not like I could ask me anything I didn't already know the answer to. But I needed to break the silence.

"Well, it's been nice talking with you," I said.

"Same, here. Sort of . . ."

"Yeah, sort of . . ." I reached to end the call.

The phone rang.

It was me, again.

"I gotta go," I said. "I'm getting a call from me."

"Me, too," he said.

"Later . . . ?"

"Probably."

"Bye," I said to me.
I took the other call. "Hi," I said to me.
"Who's this?"
"You'll figure it out," I said.
Good thing I had unlimited calling.

THE RUNNING OF
THE HOUNDS

I like almost everything we do in my Young Adventurers Group. I love hiking and fishing, and I'm pretty good at knots. Cooking is fun, too. But I'm really not a fan of Campfire Creep-Out. I know the stories aren't real, but it's still hard to accept that the creaks, scritches, and rustles I hear around me during my walk home from the meeting are all natural. And the feeling doesn't end when I get home. Creepy thoughts chase each other through my mind until I fall asleep. And then, creepy dreams take their place.

Our regular meetings are in the basement of St. Dominic's Church, but for the Creep-Out we go up the road to Tucker's Pond, where there's a fire pit. Usually, our troop leader, Mr. Benchley, will read scary stories from a book. This time, for a change, he invited people from the neighborhood to tell us the creepy legends from their cultures.

It started out fine. Mr. Giaccomo, who runs Kevin's New York Style Pizzeria, told us about the Jersey Devil, who stalked the Pine Barrens of south Jersey. That story didn't scare me, because we're at least a thousand miles away from New Jersey, and there aren't any pine trees anywhere near here.

Ms. Patrois, who teaches French at the high school, told a Haitian story about zombies. By the time she reached the end, I could feel my muscles start to tighten.

Weird old Mr. Mackalson was up next. Nobody is sure what he does. But we've all seen him loading up his rusty ancient station wagon with cameras, binoculars, and all sorts of electronic gadgets, before driving off and disappearing for days in the mountains.

He told us about the Dread Stomper, an invisible monster who was attracted to fear and driven to stomp its victims into the ground without mercy. I think he made all of it up, because he didn't even say what country the monster was from. Still, it spooked me a lot, as I tried to imagine how anybody could escape from an invisible monster, or how you could stop your fear once you knew a Dread Stomper was on your trail.

We had three more stories after that, and then, just as Mr. Benchley was getting ready to end the meeting, Mr. Maddox, who's on the town council, raced toward us from the darkness beyond the fire pit, his eyes wide with terror, and screamed, "They're coming!"

I leaped to my feet. But when I noticed Mr. Benchley was trying to hide a smile, I realized this was all a set-up to introduce the last story with a bang. At least I wasn't the only one who'd jumped. Our whole troop was standing.

As we settled back down on the ground, Mr. Maddox charged to the fire and started his tale.

"Listen," he said, pointing toward the heavens. "Can you hear it? It's them. They're baying and howling. Snarling beasts running with the thunder, chasing down their prey as they descend from the clouds with the fury of a storm."

I listened. I didn't hear anything except the pounding of my heart.

"Gabriel Ratchets," he said. "That's what they are. Some call them *Gabriel Hounds*. And, aye, they are hounds, for sure. But not like any you'd want to meet. Or any that travel on land. They're huge, and terrible, with eyes like burning coals, and sharp teeth to tear chunks of flesh off their victims to feed their endless appetite. They could eat a whale in an eye blink. But that's not what they're hungry for."

He went on for a while, describing the dreadful fate of those the hounds hunted. He didn't explain how the victims were chosen, how often the hounds hunted, or even why dogs would live in the sky. There were plenty of gaps in the story, but he made up for that with a lot of energy and plenty of dramatic hand gestures as he told the tale. Just as he finished, a log in the firepit crackled and exploded with a bang, sending up a shower of sparks, and sending us back to our feet.

We ended the meeting without sitting down again.

"Want a ride?" one of my friends asked as we doused the fire. "I'd hate to walk home after this."

"I'm fine," I lied.

Naturally, I kept hearing the shuffling of zombie feet coming toward me from all directions as I cut across a field that bordered the pond. I could picture them slinking through the darkness, like in the movies, with their arms out and their flesh falling off their faces, hungry for my brains. That spooked me. I tried to forget about zombies, but Ms. Patrois was a really good story teller, and she managed to wedge the tale deep into my brain. I was afraid I'd spend the night sharing my bed with visions of the undead.

Then, something chased away the zombies. Thunder. It was faint and distant. But beneath the rumble, I could swear I heard the baying of a pack of hounds.

"It's just geese or something," I said. "There's no such thing as Gabriel Hounds." But I sped up as I left the field and reached the road.

The thunder grew louder and closer. So did the baying.

I tried again. "It's all in your mind." That didn't work any better than *it's just geese*.

I looked over my shoulder, and froze, as a flash of lightning illuminated the sky. Still far off, dark figures loped toward me from the clouds. As my eyes recovered from the flash, I saw pairs of red embers pierce the night. Mr. Maddox's words came back to me: *Eyes like burning coals.*

Gabriel Hounds!

They were real, and they were on my trail. I burst into a run as the rain began to fall. Home was still ten blocks away. From what Mr. Maddox had told us, I had to believe I'd be safe once I got inside. He'd said people stayed sheltered behind sturdy oak doors fastened with thick iron bars during thunderstorms to avoid the hounds. He'd added, "But woe be to the traveler who is foolish enough to get caught outside when the thunder rolls in and the hounds give chase."

Foolish traveler—that would be me. I could have gotten a ride. Instead, I was racing for my life on rain-slick roads as lightning tore the sky. When I reached the next block, I risked another glance at the pack. They were closer to me, now, and closer to the ground. I could see flashes of white as they opened their jaws to let out spine-chilling cries. I didn't pause to count the hounds, but there had to be at least twenty of them.

The ground shook, as if a truck passed by. That didn't make sense. The hounds were still in the air. And I was on narrow roads where few trucks traveled.

I kept running. I reached the playground on Maple Street. I could go left or right to get to the other side. Or I could go straight, cutting through the basketball courts and the kiddie area with the swings and slide. I went straight ahead. It would be quicker. I'd have to go through the fence by the tennis courts, but there was a gate that nobody ever bothered to lock.

At least, not until now. With the hounds even closer, I stared at the huge lock that hung from the gate handle. I turned back to face the hounds. They'd reached the ground, not far from me.

I was trapped.

I'd seen angry dogs in backyards, and a snarling guard dog at an auto scrap yard. But I'd never seen anything this fierce. They growled from deep in their throats. The rain seemed to turn to steam as it hit their backs.

The ground shook as they ran, like tiny tremors were trying to build into one large body-wrenching earthquake. Mixed with the thunderclaps and lightning flashes, it felt like the whole world was attacking me from every direction.

I spun away from the hounds and kicked at the gate. It was no use. I'd never break through. Worse, the frantic action threatened to feed my panic and push me to the point where I couldn't even think.

I forced myself to stop kicking. But I had to do something. I couldn't just give up. I grabbed the fence with both hands. I could try to climb it, but I knew the hounds would leap through the air and pull me down. I could try to do the unexpected, and run right through the pack. That didn't seem like a good plan, either.

The howls and snarls died so suddenly, the change was as startling as a thunderclap. I spun back around. The hounds, no more than ten yards away, stood still, and silent, as if waiting for a signal to spring on me and tear me to pieces.

"Stop!" I shouted. "Leave me alone!"

I realized this could be my last moment on Earth. Wet, scared, and alone. That's how I'd die. I should have taken the ride. I should have tried to climb the fence, even if that gave me only a small chance to escape. But I couldn't move. As much as I tried to stay calm, I was so scared I could almost taste my terror. Above the hard splatter of the rain and the thunder in the clouds, I heard another sound. It would have been drowned out if it weren't right in front of me. But it was less than a yard away.

Crunch!

A depression appeared in the playground gravel, five feet to my left, as if a giant were lumbering toward me. The ground shook even harder.

Crunch.

A second depression appeared, about five feet to my right. The shake that came with it almost jolted me off my feet.

As if they'd finally been given a signal to act, the hounds all let out a soul-piercing howl and leaped toward me, mouths wide open. I slammed my eyes shut and braced for the impact that would come as they fell on me. If they could eat a whale in an eye blink, they could finish me off before I even knew it. At least it would be quick.

But nothing ripped my flesh.

I opened my eyes, blinking hard to clear away the raindrops that blurred my vision, and saw something stranger than everything else I'd seen on this strangest night of all. The hounds dangled in the air, as if they'd struck an invisible shield.

No. It wasn't a shield. It was their target. They sank their claws into some invisible mass. Teeth snapped as they bit into their prey. Heads jerked sharply to the side as they tore off chunks of flesh. A stench of rotten meat washed over me, as if the hounds had ripped open a road-killed carcass.

But this was no carcass. They were battling the Dread Stomper. It might have been invisible, but it was as real as the hounds. I could see its bulk, where the rain struck its body and rolled off.

It spun, trying to fling off the hounds, and brushed me with one massive, thrashing arm, knocking me hard against the fence. I could feel the padlock press against my spine. The hounds held on. I heard another crunch. The hounds were suddenly lower. The creature must have dropped to its knees. I slipped along the side of the fence, away from the gate, hoping to be out of the way when the monster fell.

And fall it did, with one final ground-shaking crunch. The hounds swarmed around their prey, devouring the invisible monster from all sides.

They made quick work of it. And then, before I realized that this feast had been my chance to escape, they all faced me.

"Thank you," I said, hoping that the monster they'd brought down wasn't just a warm-up for the hounds.

One of them, at the head of the pack, seemed to nod, but maybe that was just my imagination. I was still trembling all over, making it hard to focus on what I saw.

The hounds loped away, then leaped in the air and didn't

touch the ground again. I watched them run toward the clouds. After they'd passed out of sight, I walked along the fence until I reached the sidewalk. I was shaking and sweating. But I realized I wasn't shaking from fear, anymore. My nerves were buzzing from the remains of a narrow escape.

No zombies or other horrors followed me as I walked the last stretch toward home. I think the hounds had slayed them, too. No monsters haunted my dreams. But the hounds roamed through them, guarding me in my sleep that night, and many nights since. No story ever scared me again. No nightmare ever troubled me. But I knew, the next time Campfire Creep-Out came around, I could spin a tale that would chill your blood, freeze your heart, and haunt your dreams.

A BOY AND HIƧ FROG

I guess I was about five when I got Jumparoony. Dad found the tiny frog in the backyard after a heavy rainstorm. Nobody expected him to last long. Especially when he was being taken care of by a little kid. Actually, at first it didn't even look like I'd get to keep him.

"You aren't letting that slimy thing in my house," Mom said, making a face like she'd bitten into a caterpillar.

"Oh come on," Dad said, "the kid needs a pet."

They argued for a while. From what I remember, the discussion leaped quickly off the subject of the frog and bounced into other areas like Dad's love of bowling and Mom's shopping habits. I never did understand the rules grown-ups used when they argued about stuff. But the end result worked out fine for me.

Once Dad had talked Mom into letting me keep the frog, he warned me not to get upset if the frog croaked. Well, he didn't say it that way, and if he had I wouldn't have gotten the joke, but I remember him explaining that frogs usually didn't last as long as cats or dogs.

The thing is, this frog must not have known that he was supposed to die. He just kept on living. And he kept on growing. Within a year, he'd grown to about the size of a baseball, except of course a baseball doesn't have legs. Or bulging eyes. But if you imagined him rolled up, that's about the size he'd have been.

I really didn't have a clue why he did so well. Maybe I was just good at taking care of pets. Mom says everyone has gifts. I guess I had a special touch with animals. That's the only way I can explain things.

I had Jumpy—that's what I called him those days—for almost five years then, and during that time, he kept on growing. From the size of a baseball, he grew to the size of a softball. At that point, I could still pick him up without any trouble, but parts of him would spill over the sides of my hand.

Then he swelled up to the size of a bowling ball. I started needing two hands to lift him. Once he reached the size of a basketball, I definitely needed both hands. He felt like one of those extra-large water balloons.

He was eating a lot, too. I guess you need plenty of food when you're growing that much. It wasn't a problem at first. He did a great job keeping the house free of flies. As long as he stayed inside, there was nothing to worry about. But he got out through the kitchen window one morning and headed straight into the yard next door. Our neighbor, Mrs. Munswinger, used to have five Chihuahuas. Now she has four.

It was an amazing thing to see. Those five annoying little dogs—looking a lot like nervous rats—were huddled together barking at Jumpy. He just sat there calmly for a moment, then he flicked out his tongue and snatched one of the dogs. The Chihuahua went flying through the air so fast it didn't even have time to let out more than a little yip of surprise before it disappeared head-first down Jumpy's wide mouth. Slurp. Its curled tail vanished last, passing through Jumpy's lips like a dangling strand of spaghetti.

I dashed over and tried to scoop up my frog. I really couldn't lift all of him off the ground, but I was able to get enough of a grip so I could slide him back toward our yard. Beneath my left hand, I thought I could feel something kicking weakly in his stomach, but I wasn't sure and I really didn't want to think about it. The four surviving dogs just sat there shivering. It was the only time I'd seen them go quiet.

I dragged Jumpy back to the house. Once we got inside, he followed me up the steps to my room. "We're in big trouble," I told him. "There's got to be a law against eating Chihuahuas."

He looked back at me, blinked a couple times, then let out a small burp. Apparently, he wasn't concerned.

Fortunately, Mrs. Munswinger never caught on. She cried and wailed about her missing darling, her poor dear Mibsey, who was lost and gone forever, but she never cast a suspicious eye in my direction.

The next time Jumpy got loose, I caught him right before he hopped into the yard on the other side. That would have been a disaster. Mrs. Hildegarde runs this day care thing in her house, and there are usually a half dozen babies crawling around the yard, eating handfuls of dirt and stabbing at each other with sticks. Most of them are bigger than a Chihuahua, but they're still pretty small.

"This can't go on," I told Jumpy.

He looked at me with that frog expression that seems wise and silly at the same time.

"I have to release you back into the wild. That's the right thing to do." I'd been watching a lot of nature movies on the Disney Channel, so I knew all about setting wild animals free. I took a deep breath. It wasn't going to be easy. "I'll miss you, buddy."

I led Jumpy to the garage and dragged out my old wagon. He was definitely way too big and squishy for me to lift, now. "Come on, boy, get in," I said, patting the wagon and trying to sound like we were about to have an adventure. "Come on. Good boy."

He jumped right up and settled into the bottom of the wagon like a bucketful of pudding. I pulled him along the driveway and out to the sidewalk.

"My word, what is that?" Mrs. Munswinger asked as I walked past her yard.

I glanced down at the wagon. Jumpy's eyes were closed and his legs were tucked underneath his body, so it really was hard to see any shape. "Mom's cleaning out the fridge," I said. "This was in the back. Want some?"

"No!" She turned pale and backed away from me, holding her hands out like she'd seen a monster.

I headed off. It was a long way to Bear Creek Swamp. I ran into a couple more people, but they just stared at the wagon and didn't ask any questions. When I got to the swamp, I said, "Come on, Jumpy, here's your new home."

He just sat there. Finally, I tipped the wagon over and spilled him onto the ground.

"See ya . . . ," I said. That was all I could manage to choke out. I took one last look at him, then turned and ran off, pulling the wagon behind me.

I missed him. It would be hard to imagine that any kid ever

had a better frog. But there were just too many small dogs and little children in the neighborhood. Things would have gotten out of hand.

It was about two years later when I first heard folks discussing the sudden drop in the bird population in Bear Creek Swamp. After that, it was rabbits and squirrels. A couple years later, most of the deer vanished. There were a lot of theories. Everyone tried to explain it. None of the explanations made much sense, but the plain fact was that there was a lot less wildlife in the swamp than people thought there should be. Once, the area had been filled with deer. Now, a deer was a rare sight.

I realized that things were on their way to getting out of control. Once the deer were gone, Jumpy would probably start on the bears—Bear Creek Swamp wasn't given that name for no reason. But once the bears were gone, along with the rest of the wildlife, I could just imagine Jumpy wandering out of the swamp and into some place where there were lots of people.

I had to try to restore the natural order of things. I couldn't let Jumpy wipe out all life in the swamp. But I didn't want to do anything to hurt him. There had to be another way. He'd started out eating flies. Maybe that was the answer. If I'd raised one giant pet, I figured I should be able to raise another. So I poured a blob of honey on a piece of paper and put it down in the backyard. Then I waited with a jar until some flies landed.

I snuck up on the flies, slammed down the jar, and caught a bunch of them on the first try. I brought them up to my room and started taking care of them. I guess flies aren't supposed to live very long, either. But these did. And they grew.

One fly, especially, started getting real big real fast. I named her Buzzella.

After a week, Buzzella was as big as a bumblebee. In two weeks, she was the size of a sparrow. In a month, she was as large as a vulture. I kept her in an old bird cage I'd found in the basement. Soon, I needed to find more cages as the other flies caught up with her.

I'll say one thing—as much as a kid is supposed to love his pets, I'd be the first to admit that a fly that size was about as ugly as anything I'd ever seen. And I had a hard time looking her in the eyes. Every time I did, I'd see a million reflections of my guilty face. I felt rotten because I was raising her for one purpose—she and her friends were going to be frog food.

After three months, I took Buzzella and the rest of the flies out to the swamp. I set them loose and watched as they flew off in-between the trees. All I could do now was hope that they'd produce lots more flies.

I guess it worked.

It's been three years since I set the flies loose. The wildlife made a comeback. But people don't go into Bear Creek Swamp anymore. After the first few reports of giant flies, everyone learned to stay away. At least the trouble hasn't spread. Whatever is happening, it's just happening in the swamp. So far.

As for me, I'm happy that the flies haven't gotten out of control. Everything is back in balance. My life would be perfect right now except for one tiny thing. Well, actually, a lot of tiny things. Yesterday, for my birthday, my dad gave me an ant farm. I have a funny feeling those four dogs next door aren't out of danger yet.

BLACK FRIDAY

In a land where nearly all the residents had glutted themselves on turkey, stuffing, gravy, and an abundance of other traditional Thanksgiving foods and fixings, midnight approached. This was the promised evening that was the most exciting, rewarding, and important night of the year for some.

"Black Friday is almost upon us," Alba's mother said.

"Why do they call it that?" Alba asked. She knew the answer, but she loved to hear her mother tell tales. Her mother dabbled in poetry, and fancied herself something of a writer.

"Because, dearest daughter, this is the day the stores make their first profit. All year, they've worked to pay off their expenses. There are a large number of costs connected with owning a business. Tonight, the crowds will swarm to the stores. So many people will shop, so much money will flow, that the profits brought in will finally exceed the money the merchants have spent on salaries, supplies, and rent. Losses are written in red ink, as if blood itself were spilled. Profit is written in black. And so, today is Black Friday, beginning at the stroke of midnight."

Alba waited. She knew there was more, but she was patient. She savored the silence before the best part.

Her mother continued. "Black ink. That's what some people say. Others feel that this is the day when the human heart is at its blackest. Neighbor tramples neighbor for a sweater or a purse. Friend pushes friend aside to save pennies on the price of an unneeded item."

"If it's so dark and evil, why are we going?" Alba asked.

Her mother smiled. "Because there are bargains to be had and treasures to be seized."

Alba and her mother approached the mall as midnight drew near. They were far from the first to queue up by the main entrance. People had lined up hours ago for a chance to be the first through the door. The mall had five entrances, but the largest crowd was in front of Dresher's, a department store known for its Black Friday bargains. More shoppers soon stepped in behind Alba, adding to the mass of bargain hunters.

"It's sad that people have to work so late." Alba looked up at the stars. "Or is it so early?"

"Sad for them, good for us," her mother said. "And *late* or *early* all depends on when they started."

Alba studied the mob. She was skilled at reading people. So was her mother, who narrated a description of actions around them in whispered tones meant for only one pair of ears. "See them? Excitement and fear. That's what's coursing through their veins and pulsing through their minds. They are excited by the thought of bargains." She paused.

Alba filled in the rest. "And afraid someone else will snatch their bargains away."

"There will be scuffles," her mother said. "We'll stay safely clear of them. What's the rule?"

"Never attract attention," Alba said. She studied the people closest to them. She was pleased nobody was even looking at her or her mother, and she was positive nobody who did look at them would guess they came not to buy but to steal.

"That's my girl," her mother said. "Never stand out. Never be memorable." Her head turned sharply, as if she'd heard something significant.

Alba heard it, too. The clack of a bolt being thrown open. A door unlatched. The mob pressed forward, pushing against the very doors that needed to swing outward to admit them.

"See. They fight against their own best interest," Alba's mother said.

"I see."

"It would be so much easier if they cooperated."

Life was a lesson for Alba. All of life. Her mother took every opportunity to teach her about the joys and perils of existence. That was good. Alba had a deep thirst for knowledge, perfectly matched with her mother's deep hunger to pass along her wisdom.

Swept toward the mall by the sea of flesh, they reached the entrance. The night was still dark, but no longer silent. All the primal sounds of humanity rose from the crowd. Excitement. Anger. Sorrow. Joy.

"I got it!"

"That was mine!"

"Stop pushing!"

"Look, I see the headphones!"

"You stepped on my foot!"

"They're sold out . . ."

"Jewelry," Alba's mother whispered to her. "We'll find our treasure there."

Alba was still balancing her love of solitude with the thrilling sensory overload that came from being at the center of this frenzied collection of flesh and blood. She took her mother's hand. She wasn't afraid, but she felt the need to remain in contact with the only one in the mall who wasn't caught up in the madness.

They pushed their way toward the jewelry department.

Unlike socks and scarves, the gold bracelets and diamond pendants couldn't be heaped in bins for shoppers to grab. The precious metals and gems were locked behind glass cases. Three harried clerks stood on the other side of the counter, trying to serve three dozen customers who clamored for their attention.

Alba stopped at a spot where she could both study the crowd and watch her mother study them. She still had much to learn.

"Who?" her mother asked, testing her.

Alba chose carefully. "Him?" she said, pointing at an angry man on the fringe of the mob, who looked like he was about to start lifting people up and tossing them out of his way.

"Well chosen," her mother said. "Watch him. This will be interesting."

She watched. The man barged forward with the aggressiveness of someone who lived his life as if others had no feelings. Or even as if others weren't real. He reached the counter and stole the attention of one clerk away from a young woman who, like Alba's mother, also had a daughter in tow.

Alba watched the man purchase a necklace that, though deeply discounted, was still absurdly expensive.

"How precious," her mother said.

"He must love someone," Alba said.

"Just himself," her mother said.

Alba was sure her mother was right about that.

The clerk put the necklace in a hinged box covered with black velvet. She put the box in a bag, and the bag in the man's hand. The instant his fingers met the bag, he snatched it from the clerk and clutched it to his chest, as if he were afraid it would be stolen. Hunching his shoulders to further guard his treasure, he pressed against the tide of shoppers as he left the counter and forced his way toward a clear aisle.

"What will he be driving?" Alba's mother asked her as they followed the man toward the exit.

"Something fancy and expensive," Alba said. "So the world will know he's important."

"Right. And where will he park?"

Alba thought about what she'd learned over the years. "Either as close as possible to the entrance, because he's lazy and he feels entitled, or far off, so nobody will dent his door with theirs."

"So, will it be close or far?" her mother asked.

Alba studied the man. He was strong and lean. "Far. He's in good shape. He won't mind walking. He's probably a jogger."

Her mother rewarded her with a fond squeeze on the shoulder. "Very good, my dear."

They followed the man across the main lot, and then across an access road, all the way to the farthest row of the overflow lot. His car, very expensive and very red, was parked at a slant, taking up two spaces.

"Other people don't matter to him, do they?" Alba asked. She felt she had to justify what they were about to do.

"No. He only sees himself. Others are just paper cutouts to him. They exist for his benefit. He's a taker." She smiled at Alba. "It's our turn to take."

As the man reached out to open the car door, Alba's mother moved with the natural speed of her kind. It was a speed that would be a blur to human eyes. She took the man down before he could utter a cry, or even a gasp, muffling his mouth and nose with one hand, pulling down the collar of his coat with the other, exposing his neck.

She offered her daughter first blood. Alba was happy to accept the gift. She'd been waiting a long time for it.

"We found a bargain," her mother said, after both of them had drank their fill.

Alba wiped a small spill of blood from her chin with her handkerchief. The blood, pumped rich with adrenalin and oxygen from the thrill of the victorious battle for a bargain, was especially satisfying. There was nothing like it. Her whole body buzzed in a good way from the experience. "I love Red Friday," she said.

"Black Friday," her mother said.

"Maybe to them," Alba said, pointing across the road toward the mall, where cries of triumph and rage still echoed as the humans continued their hunt for bargains. "But not to us."

"You're right, my dear," her mother said. "For us, it's Red Friday. Always and forever."

ROMEO, ROMEO, WHEREFLOOR ARGLE ROBLIO?

It was Karzoy's idea. He came up with it while I was whupping him severely at Arena Duel. His gladiator had already lost an arm and part of one foot. Victory was mine. I was just getting ready to cleave his player in half from head to toe when he threw down the controller, leaped up from the floor, and shouted, "Infinite monkeys!" He clenched his fists and shook them like he'd just kicked a fifty-yard field goal. "Yes!"

"Huh?" I was coordinated enough to cleave him as originally planned, despite the interruption, and follow up with a horizontal slash at waist level while I spoke.

"You know—Mr. Cantor told us about it in math class last year. If infinite monkeys typed at infinite typewriters, they'd produce all the works of Shakespeare."

"What's the point?" I hit the button to replay Karzoy's death in slow motion, and captured the video for later viewing pleasure and massive sharing. "We already have all the works of Shakespeare. I don't see why we'd want some monkeys to type them up all over again. Seems like a total waste of good monkeys."

"But we don't have our essays," he said.

Okay. Now he sort of had my attention, though the magnificent gore on the screen was hard to tear myself away from. We were only in sixth grade, but Ms. Fezniak, who, along with Mr. Adamola and Mrs. Epstein, made up our teaching team, decided it wasn't too early for her students to learn the joys of writing a ten-page paper. Yeah. Ten pages. With footnotes.

"We don't have any monkeys," I said. "And I don't think anyone has a typewriter, except for my uncle Andy. He's got one in the basement. I'm pretty sure it doesn't work. There's about an inch of dust on it."

"We don't need monkeys," Karzoy said. "It's the principle that's important. If you bang at a keyboard for long enough, you'll produce every possible thing that could be written. Including a totally awesome essay."

"You mean, two essays," I said. "Right? Whatever you're planning can't work just once. It has to work for each of us."

"For sure. If it works at all, it can work infinite times. So are you in on this?" he asked.

"Yeah. Why not? What's the worst that could happen?" I have, since then, learned that there are some questions better left untested.

Karzoy's total lack of skill in the arena with a halberd or pike is made up for by the fact that he's a bit of a computer genius. Though, smart as he is, he's not big on writing papers. Which, I guess, is why he'd been searching for a way out while I'd been searching for ways to hack through his defense. I guess that made both of us hackers.

His real name is a lot longer, and pretty much spelled without much help from vowels, but it sounds sort of like what you'd get if you said "Karzoy," while in the middle of a violent sneeze that was, itself, in the middle of a string of violent hiccups. I'm a bit of a computer idiot. I'm not big on writing papers, either. And my name, whether or not you are sneezing, is simply Liam. But Karzoy and I have been pals for ages.

We got right to work. This meant Karzoy started coding, and I hovered behind him, trying to make sense of what he was doing.

"There are twenty-six letters," Karzoy said. "So there are twenty-six times twenty-six possible pairs of letters. And twenty-six times more if you add a third letter. Actually twenty-seven, if you include spaces and ignore punctuation. Get it?"

"Sure." I sort of got that. Though I had a funny feeling I would soon be switching from *sure* to *huh* as he tried to explain things to me.

"A pathetic, bumbling patzer would start with that sort of brute-force approach," he said. "But starting with letters is unproductive and unnecessary, unless your goal is to compile reams of gibberish."

This was already close to sounding like gibberish. Though I'd learned from him a while ago that a "patzer" was a bad chess player. Which I happened to be. My board game skills had peaked somewhere between Candy Land and checkers.

"Letters are out," Karzoy said, continuing the lecture. "It makes more sense to start with . . ."

He gave me the sort of expectant look one offers a puppy after saying, "Sit!" I guess he wanted to make sure I was following along by asking me to fill in the blank.

"Words?" I guessed.

"Exactly!" He thumped the table with his hand. "However,

there are about half a million words in English. So the possible combinations for two words would be . . ."

"Half a million times half a million," I said, surprised I was still an active participant in the conversation.

"Right! The possible number of combinations gets staggering almost immediately, and soon surpasses all the molecules in our solar system. We'd have to wait centuries for anything that resembled an essay, even if we tapped into the fastest processers available or crowd-sourced the task."

"We don't have centuries. Or even weeks. The essays are due next Friday," I said.

"I know. But this is where it gets to be fun. We can filter everything through grammar rules, and toss out anything that fails to parse properly," Karzoy said. "I'll admit, that's a pretty obvious solution. Anyone would think of it. Right?"

"Uh, yeah. Right. Sure," I said. "But you have a better idea?"

Karzoy grinned like he'd just invented both ice cream and hot caramel sauce in one furious burst of inspiration. And, maybe, crushed peanuts. "I figured out that I can combine hermeneutics with a bit tree pruning. And let the AI digest the sample papers she gave us." He grabbed a stack of essays and put them in his scanner. Then, he resumed typing.

I waited. I knew an explanation was coming. I didn't understand most of it, but I got the two main points. Karzoy was going to let the program learn what qualified as a good sentence, and then a paragraph, and then an essay. On top of that, he'd have the program compare what it created against the massive supply of essays that already existed on the Internet.

"We don't want to produce something that's already been written," he said. "We'd get in trouble. They check for that.

All the teachers do. We just want something as acceptable as what's been written. And something that follows the basic structure of essays that Ms. Fezniak likes."

He typed for another five minutes, then spun around in his chair, threw up another fist pump, and said, "Done! It's running. We'll have our papers by Wednesday or Thursday, at the latest."

"Are you sure?" I asked. If he was wrong, I'd be writing an entire essay Thursday evening. Not that I hadn't done things like that before.

"Positive," he said. "Let's make good use of our free time. I want a rematch."

So we played—proving that even the smartest kids don't learn certain lessons—and goofed off, and smirked at our classmates when they talked about the hours they were spending on their papers.

On Wednesday afternoon, Karzoy took me into his room, and said, "It's ready."

"Our papers?"

"Yup." He tapped a key, and the printer hummed to life. Soon after that, he handed me my paper.

"Better read it," he said. "Just in case Ms. Fezniak doesn't believe you wrote it."

"Good idea." I sat on Karzoy's bed and read my essay. "Hey, this is pretty good," I said when I was finished. "You really did it! You *are* a genius."

Karzoy smiled and shrugged. "Thanks."

He printed out a second copy for each of us. That was part of the assignment. We had to send a file to our school account, but we also had to turn in two printed copies. I had no idea why, and didn't really care.

We handed in our papers on Friday. On Monday morning, Ms. Fezniak handed back the papers. Each student got one copy, with a grade and hand-written comments.

But not us. I looked at Karzoy when it was obvious he and I were the only ones who didn't get our papers back.

"What's going on?" I asked him at lunch.

"No idea," he said.

"Are you sure they aren't the same as some real paper?" I asked. That was the only explanation I could think of for not getting the papers back.

"Positive," Karzoy said. "They absolutely do not exist in any online data base. I checked."

At the end of the day, right before the bell rang, Ms. Fezniak told me and Karzoy to remain seated.

I expected her to accuse us of cheating. I was prepared to get some sort of punishment, and to act like I was sorry. I didn't expect the police to show up.

"Burglary is a serious crime," one of the officers said.

I couldn't even think of an answer.

"And copying two of my old papers was not a smart move," Ms. Fezniak said. "I don't know how you got into my home, but I am horrified at your actions."

"But . . . ," I said. I had no words. I glanced over at Karzoy. He was speechless, too. We could really have used some of those monkeys, now. It turned out that even though there are zillions of papers online, there are way more that aren't on the Internet. Including many of the student papers Ms. Fezniak had saved from her thirty years of teaching. I guess that's why she wanted two copies. She gave one back with comments and a grade, and kept one for herself. It was our bad luck that our infinite monkeys had spewed out a pair of papers that were way too close to two of the ones in Ms. Fezniak's collection. Later, Karzoy told me the odds against this were so astronomical as to be virtually impossible, even though he'd used a couple real papers to help train the software. I told him the odds were meaningless when I was involved, and that bad luck was virtually inevitable. If things could go bad for me, they would.

In the end, we confessed about the software. It was better to get punished for cheating than for burglary. And we still had to write our essays. On top of that, the school and our parents decided community service would be a good punishment. We had to spend fifty hours picking up litter in the park, jabbing it with a stick and stuffing it in a garbage bag. I never realized what a diverse and disgusting assortment of things people threw on the ground.

"You know, we could make robots to do this," Karzoy said, halfway into our first hour. "Small ones. We could sneak them into the park and let them do the work. The basic cybernetic—"

I smacked him with the blunt end of my stick. He's pretty bad at combat in the real world, too. But, at least, I didn't slice him in half. Not that I didn't want to.

MY FAMILY HISTORY

Christopher, can I see you for a minute," my teacher, Mrs. Woolrich, asked as the bell rang at the end of the day.

"Uh, sure." My heart raced. And a tingle ran down my spine.

"Don't worry. You aren't in trouble," she said.

"That's good." I felt my tongue flick at my upper lip. I do that when I'm nervous. I walked up to her desk, and spotted my essay lying there. It didn't have any marks on it. No grade or comments or anything. But she must have read it. Otherwise, she wouldn't have wanted to talk to me.

Mrs. Woolrich picked up the essay. "I'd like to ask you some questions about this."

I nodded, and waited. I'd felt great when I'd handed it in. I thought I'd done a really good job, and had totally followed the directions.

"You know this was supposed to be about your real family," she said.

"Yeah. I know."

"It wasn't a story assignment," she said. "We finished our

fiction lessons last week. I wanted you to write about your real family, this time."

"I did."

"I know you're new here, but it's important, when we're writing an essay, to stick with the truth."

"I did," I said. I knew about sticking to the truth. I'd been to a bunch of schools, and they all had that same rule. They had other rules, too, that were really important to follow.

"Your father and mother are bears?" she asked, tapping the second line of my essay.

"Big ones," I said. I raised my arms and growled like a bear. That was fun, because it was so far from the truth.

She tapped the first paragraph. "They're grizzly bears, and you all live in a cave near Folsom's Woods?"

"Yup."

"And they make you sleep on the hard stone floor of the cave?" she asked.

"It's not that bad," I said. "I'm used to it. It's nice and cool."

"All you get to eat are berries?"

"I like berries," I said. "That's what bears eat."

"It doesn't sound like a very good situation for a child." She pulled her phone out of her purse. "Maybe I should give your parents a call so we can discuss this in person."

"We don't have a phone. Dad doesn't trust them. He says they're too modern."

"Everyone has a phone," she said.

"His paws are too big to use the keyboard," I said. "And he's so strong, he'd crush the screen. Mom's paws are huge, too."

Mrs. Woolrich put the phone back in her purse. "Well, maybe I should come out to your house—"

"Cave," I said.

"Okay, your cave, and pay your parents a visit."

"I don't think they'd like that," I said. "They're very busy."

"That doesn't matter. I'm sure they'll make time," she said. "I have a meeting to go to, right now. But later on, I'm paying your parents a visit. Tell them I'll be there after dinner."

"I will." I waited to see if there was anything else she wanted to say.

"You can go," she said.

"Thanks." I headed out. My parents weren't bears, of course. Bears are lowly mammals, with no ability to read or write, and their cubs don't go to school. The thought of that made me laugh.

"I'm home," I said when I got to our house, which definitely wasn't a cave. We'd rented it, but only for a month, since we had no plans to stay around. I was still laughing at the idea of a bear cub going to school.

Mom met me on the porch. "How'd it go?"

I paused by the entrance, unzipped my boy suit, and enjoyed the feeling of afternoon sunlight warming my scales. "She totally fell for it."

"Wonderful," Mom said. "When will she be coming?"

"After dinner," I said.

"After *her* dinner," Mom said. She hissed out a laugh and flicked her tongue across her lips.

"And right in time for ours," Dad said as he joined us.

We all laughed at that. We might be cold-blooded killer lizards who sneaked among the humans and used them for food, without feeling bad at all about doing it, but we did have a sense of humor.

WHEN DEATH
COMES CALLING

I was asleep when my bedroom door creaked open.

A figure stood at the entrance, backlit by the night light in the hallway. I couldn't see his face. He appeared to be wearing a robe with a hood and long sleeves. He was holding a sickle in his hand. The blade brushed the top of the door frame.

This is not going to be a good dream, I thought as my eyes opened wider than I believed possible.

He stepped inside, making no creak on the spot where my floor always creaks.

I sat up and switched on my lamp.

The light revealed a man's face inside the hood. No grinning skull. No empty eye sockets. He looked like someone who could sell men's cologne in a TV commercial. Handsome or not, he still held a weapon that could dish out a lot of damage. I inched back toward the corner where my headboard met the wall, and tried to accept the impossible truth that this wasn't a dream at all.

I fought down the urge to scream. I didn't think anything

good would come of bringing my parents running into the room. Or my little sister.

"Who are you?" I asked.

He stared at me like that was the stupidest question in the world.

Black robe with hood, sickle, silent footsteps. The answer was obvious.

"You're Death?" I said. My voice broke on the second word, creaking like the door.

He nodded.

To my surprise, my first thought wasn't to plead for mercy or make a dash for the hallway. My first thought was the small happiness that came from knowing he wasn't here for someone else in my family.

Wait.

That wasn't necessarily true.

"Did you come just for me?" I asked.

"Relax, Thomas," he said. His voice was deep and soft. "I'm not here for that."

"You're not?"

"Nope."

"Honestly?" I'd read stories where Death tricked people in all sorts of ways.

"Honestly." He started to drag his finger across his chest. "Cross my heart and hope to . . ."

He let the hand drop, and smirked as if he realized how strange it would be to finish that sentence. But at least I pretty much believed him, now. He wasn't going to take me away.

"So why are you here?"

"Sometimes, even Death needs a little help." He reached into a pocket of his robe and pulled out a phone. He had the long, slender fingers of someone who could make playing cards disappear and coins multiply right before your eyes. "I heard you're good with these."

"I'm great." I felt a jolt of fear as the words left my lips. Bragging to Death seemed like a good way to make bad things happen. Though what I said was true. I was awesome with operating systems, and pretty good with hardware. I could hack the unhackable and repair the irreparable. Everyone has a knack for something. That was mine. I could fix almost anything that went wrong with most phones, tablets, and even laptops.

He held out the phone. It was a new model that had just hit the stores last month, with the ultra-strong glass and the modifiable interface.

"See what you can do with this," he said.

I reached out, making sure our fingers didn't meet. I guess he noticed.

"I'm not contagious," he said.

"Sorry."

"My touch isn't lethal."

"Good to know."

"I'm just doing my job. I'm good at it."

"I know the feeling." I switched on the phone. It was stuck in the middle of a system update.

"Can you fix it?" he asked.

"Probably." I tried doing a hard reset, but it didn't respond. "I'm going to have to open it up."

"Do what you have to," he said. "Try not to kill it."

I stared at him. He shrugged. "That was a joke."

I got my electronics tool kit from the middle drawer of my

desk. I figured the best bet was to pull the battery. Five minutes later, I had the phone back in working order. Ten minutes after that, I finished installing the update.

"Fixed?" he asked.

"Almost. I want to check whether any of your apps was damaged."

As I was testing the phone to make sure everything worked, I opened his calendar. There were five names on his list for tonight. My stomach clenched as I recognized one of them. *Wilbur Cutgreve.*

Oh, no! Not him.

Mr. Cutgreve was this nice old guy who lived on the next block over. I'd known him for as long as I could remember. He was as much a part of the neighborhood as the giant willow tree in our front yard, or the red fire hydrant on the corner. He loved decorating his house for all the holidays. Whenever we got a lot of snow, he paid me and my friends to shovel his driveway. In the summer, he was always sitting on his porch, playing dominoes or gin rummy with his next door neighbor, Mr. Vishner.

He had one of those ancient flip phones. It never needed to be fixed. But it always needed to be found. Half the time I went over there, he asked me to call him, so he could track down the phone. That was easy, even if it was all the way across the house, or in the backyard, since the ringer was set as loud as possible.

"I'm sure everything is fine," Death said. "I don't even use most of those apps."

The voice startled me back to the present. I guess I'd gotten lost in memories.

"Yeah, all fixed," I said as I handed the phone back to him.

He glanced at the screen, with the open calendar. "Thank you."

I almost said *any time*. But I didn't want to encourage Death to be a regular visitor. So I just nodded and said, "No problem."

He slipped away, as silent going out as he'd been coming in, except for the creak of the door. The instant he was gone I grabbed my phone and called Mr. Cutgreve. I wanted to warn him to get out of the house. The phone rang, unanswered, until the voicemail message cut in. I pictured Mr. Cutgreve in his bed, eyes open but seeing nothing.

"You work fast," I said. I guess Death didn't travel like the rest of us.

I wasn't able to fall back to sleep that night.

The next day, I heard the bad news I knew was coming. Mr. Cutgreve was dead. That's what I'd expected, and what I'd braced myself for. Mr. Vishner had stopped by in the morning, and gotten worried when nobody answered his knock. He'd called the police after looking through the window and seeing the body on the floor. That part, I hadn't expected. Mr. Cutgreve hadn't died in his bed. He'd died after he'd fallen down the stairs in the middle of the night. They didn't know why.

I did. He'd left his phone downstairs.

He'd stumbled in the dark when he'd tried to answer my call.

The words I'd heard in my room last night came back to me: *Sometimes, even Death needs a little help.*

I'd been used for more than just fixing a phone. Death had called on me. And I had called my neighbor to his death.

2D OR NOT 2D

There's a mad scientist in my neighborhood. I found that out when I knocked on his door, in search of more customers. It took him a long time to come to the door. I was about to give up and move on when he opened it. The *scientist* part was the first half of *mad scientist* I figured out. It wasn't hard. He was wearing a lab coat and holding a beaker. The *mad* part showed up soon enough. Though *highly enthusiastic* might be more accurate, and less judgmental.

"Want your lawn mowed?" I asked, pointing at the mess of weeds and grasses on his front yard. "I can give you a good price."

"Why bother? It will just grow back. But you're hired! Come on. There's a lot of work to do."

He grabbed my arm and yanked me inside the house. A lifetime of training about not getting into dangerous situations almost made me break free of his grip. But he let go as soon as we were inside, and said, "Do you know how to alphabetize?"

"Uh, yeah. . . ." I wasn't expecting that sort of question. "Why?"

"I have book, magazines, and journals that need to be arranged. I've no time for that. I'll pay you." He mentioned an hourly rate. It was a lot more than I'd get for cutting grass. Did I mention it was ninety-seven degrees outside, and wonderfully cool in the house?

"Deal," I said. "Where are the books?"

"Pick a room," he said, waving at various doors and corridors that led from the hallway. "Do the books by author, and the magazines by title, sorted by publication date, of course."

"Got it." I picked a room. It might have been a living room, but it was hard to tell. There were a lot of books overflowing from boxes. And there were plenty of bookcases and magazine holders.

I got to work. The books were on all sorts of sciences. So were the magazines. Who would have ever guessed there'd be a *Journal of Nanotechnology* and a *Nanotechnology Weekly*? After two hours of hard work, I figured I'd take a break. I also wanted to see whether he was planning to pay me each day, or at the end of the week.

He wasn't in any of the rooms on the first floor. But I was happy to see there was enough work to last me a good part of the summer.

I followed a zapping electronic sound up to the second floor, and found him in a room where two walls were lined with worktables. A device in the center of the room looked like the world's largest microscope. The bottom lens perched over a table. He stood next to it, fiddling with a series of dials on the side of the device.

"What's that?" I asked.

He spun, and seemed startled by my voice. I guess he'd been deep in thought. But he recovered quickly, and let out a yelp of joy. "I'll show you!"

He waved me over.

"Everyone is exploring three-D," he said. "Movies, printers, lots of applications. But do you know how to make the greatest discoveries?"

I wasn't even going to try to guess at an answer. "How?"

"Go the other way!" He shouted that like it was the punchline of the best joke in the world.

"Uh, okay. . . ." I waited for a bit more of an explanation.

"I'm working on making things two dimensional!"

"Why?"

"Why?" He seemed shocked by the question. "There are a thousand reasons. Think for yourself."

I thought for myself. Then, I thought some more. He seemed ready to wait as long as it took. This was summer, school was out, and I figured I was on a break from thinking, but I really didn't want to let him down. He reminded me of my uncle.

"Stuff would be smaller," I said.

"Yes! That's a good one." He seemed delighted at my answer. Now, he reminded me of some of my teachers. "For example, you could carry an entire first aid kit in your shirt pocket."

"But would it work?" I asked.

"That's the catch," he said. "Sometimes, it does. Sometimes, it doesn't. But I've had an encouraging number of great successes."

He went to a table, pulled open a drawer, and handed me

a flat piece of plastic about the size of a playing card. It seemed familiar, but it took me a second to realize what it was.

"A water pistol?" I asked.

"Exactly." He tapped his chest. "Try it."

I pointed it at him and pulled the trigger. A flat stream of water shot out. "How?" I asked.

"Atoms and molecules are mostly empty space," he said. "I'm just gently flattening them."

He showed me several other objects he'd converted. They were all pretty cool.

"I have to get back to work," he said. "But feel free to look around. There are plenty more examples in the drawers."

"Thanks." I snooped around for a little. Then, I spotted something that looked like a scrapbook. On the cover, he'd written *Errors, Mistakes, Glitches, and Bugs*. I guess those were his notes on things that had gone wrong. I was curious what the errors might look like.

Small tabs sticking from the book were labeled for each section. I flipped to *errors*, and discovered a wonderfully bizarre collection of distorted and mangled objects. I guess it wasn't easy to get things into a two-dimensional form.

"It's sort of like putting a globe on a flat map," I said.

"Very true," he said. "That's an excellent analogy." He didn't look up. He was still fiddling with dials and adjusting levers.

Flipping past the errors, I looked at the mistakes. Most of them were unrecognizable. I moved to the next section. The glitches seemed to be things that were almost right, except for one small flaw.

I was eager to see the *bugs*, which I had assumed were caused by programming errors. I figured they'd be wonderfully weird. Right before I flipped the page, he said, "I really need to find a safer place for the bugs and other insects. Especially the dangerous ones."

I was just a little bit slow figuring out what he was talking about. By the time the meaning of *bugs and other insects* sunk in, I was staring down at a page holding three scorpions.

The flat scorpions scuttled off the page. One of them ran onto my hand. I screamed and flung the scorpion away. The book slipped from my hand. Scads of insects emerged as the book tumbled through the air and hit the wall. A fair number of them flew or scurried right at me, like they blamed me for their imprisonment.

I swatted at myself, smacking a red ant that was climbing up my leg, and discovered the worst part about two-dimensional bugs.

You can't squash them.

I'd rather not describe the next ten minutes in detail. I'd actually rather not ever think about them again. But we managed to capture most of the bugs, and slip them back into the pages of the book. Many of them had acquired little bits of my flesh to feast on during their brief period of freedom.

It's a good think I'm not allergic to bee stings or bug bites. Still, I was pretty well bitten up. As I stared at my arms, I had a thought. "A hive could hold a whole lot of flat bees, right?"

"Absolutely," he said.

"And that would help pollinate things." I remembered there'd been a shortage of bees a while ago.

"Brilliant!" he said.

I kicked out a couple other uses for flat insects.

He grabbed another journal, and opened it.

I flinched, but it was just filled with written notes. As he jotted my ideas down, he said, "You aren't quitting, are you?"

"No way. I'm sticking around. We have tons of work to do."

I realized it was a lot of fun coming up with ideas, and even more fun brainstorming with someone who shared my enthusiasm. I liked the way it felt. I guess I'd been bitten by the science bug.

MUMMY MISSES YOU

I'm pretty lucky I didn't lose my eyes. I guess I flinched right when the explosion happened, and closed them tight enough to save my vision. I wasn't so lucky about the rest of my face. That got burned pretty badly. So did my hands. I'm all bandaged up. I learned my lesson. It's really a bad idea to try to make your own fireworks. It's an especially bad idea to try to make your own fireworks when you get the instructions from the Internet.

Never again. I promise.

At least I was able to go back to school in time for the class trip. There's a science museum just across the county line, in Freeburg. I love science. I guess that's sort of obvious. Not just fireworks and things that go bang, but atoms and stars and electric motors. Anything you can experiment with or learn about.

It wasn't too long a bus ride. And I sat with my friend, Chester. He was being super nice. Which was weird. Because Chester is basically a jerk. But he's my kind of jerk. He loves to make fun of me. Which is fine, because I love to make fun of him. But ever since I nearly blew my head off, he's been nice. Everyone has.

I hadn't been to the museum in a while. I forgot how awesome it was. They have a wooly mammoth right in the entrance, next to an electric car. We started in the Elements and Minerals room, and then went to the Amphibians display.

The trouble began when we went to the Ancient Civilizations wing. There was a mummy behind a display window, standing in an open and upright sarcophagus. The sign said it was a female, from around three thousand years ago. Everyone jumped when she moved.

"Pretty cool," Chester said. "I didn't think they'd do stuff like that."

Neither did I. I expected everything to be serious. But having someone dressed as a mummy, just to scare kids, was sort of fun.

Well, it was fun until the mummy smashed the glass.

"I don't think this is a joke," I said to Chester. Actually, I said it to the empty pocket of space that had recently been occupied by my friend before he fled from the room, ahead of the pack. Everyone was screaming and fleeing.

I stifled my scream as quickly as I could. It hurt my healing face to yell. And I tried to escape with my classmates. But the mummy grabbed me from behind in a bear hug.

For ancient, long-dead, withered muscles, her arms had an iron grip. I expected that grip to shift to my neck, or maybe just snap me in half. Most of what I knew about mummies that came to life, I learned from horror movies. All of it, actually.

Instead of throttling me, the mummy turned me so I faced her. Then, she knelt, her knees crackling like a dead leaf you pull off a branch—the stubborn last leaf that refuses to fall, even after the first snow. She pulled me so close I could smell the dust and must of ages.

My *son*, she said, whispering the words directly into my mind and burying her head against my chest.

"No." I barely managed to speak the word. My mind screamed for me to break free and run. My body didn't seem able to move.

I've waited centuries. I knew you'd find me.

"Look at me," I said. I reached up and peeled the bandages from my face. It wasn't easy. But it was necessary. "I'm not like you."

She turned her face up toward me. I stared into antiquity. She stared back, silently, into the present, and into disappointment.

The grip fell slack. She edged away, and tried to return to the display. The ledge was too high for her wrapped body to navigate.

I helped her in, fearing my own bandaged fingers would puncture her ancient wrappings. But I managed to return her to the display without doing any harm to her body. Any physical harm, at least. She got back into the same position as before. Except for the shattered glass, it looked just like she had never moved at all.

Thank you.

"I hope he finds you," I said.

I will wait.

I wound the bandages back around my face, then went off to find my classmates. It was going to be fun watching what happened when everyone claimed the mummy had chased them. Eventually, they'd decide something else broke the glass, and that the rest of it was all just their imagination. There really was no other explanation they'd accept.

I'm glad I knew better. I'm glad I knew the truth, as painful as it was. I'm glad I knew my own pain would heal. And I'm glad it wouldn't take centuries.

SEEING RED

Seriously, how long does it take to write a report? An hour? Maybe two, if you goof off too much and get distracted. Mom is constantly bugging me to do my school work as soon as I get an assignment. "Emma," she's always saying, "plan ahead." But that doesn't make any sense to me. Why should I spoil a perfectly good afternoon on one of those rare evenings when I don't have any homework due the next day?

I guess this is the long way of explaining why I was running out the front door right after dinner in search of, as my language arts teacher, Mr. Fisher, put it, *an interesting character in your neighborhood*. I'd asked if I could write about my dog, Frodo. Mr. Fisher was pretty firm about the character being human, since the assignment included an interview. So that also ruled out the owl I sometimes hear at night, the frisky squirrels that like to scamper through our trees, and the garden slugs that like to eat Dad's tomatoes. (My geeky nerd big brother, Drake, insists the owl is actually a hungry alien hunting for food by trying to lure curious kids out of their houses. He has no theories about the squirrels. I have a theory one of the slugs is responsible for laying the slimy egg from which Drake hatched. I guess that rules Drake out as an interview subject, too.)

"Did you finish your homework?" Mom called after me as I stepped onto the porch.

"Almost," I said. "I just have one more little thing to do."

I reached the sidewalk, looked left and right in search of a good subject, and asked myself, "Who?"

I had to laugh when I realized I was acting just like the owl. I said, "Who?" a couple more times, varying the pitch and volume, just for fun, then reminded myself that this wasn't getting me any closer to a finished paper.

I spent the next half hour discovering that nobody in the neighborhood had the time to let me ask some questions. Or if they had the time, they didn't have the interest. I circled my whole block in search of a subject, and then I tried the next block over. Finally, as I walked back toward my house, I saw Mrs. Muscatello across the street, a block and a half away, sweeping her sidewalk with a straw broom.

"Interesting character," I said. Nobody else in our neighborhood uses a broom. Everyone has leaf blowers, which are also perfectly suited for sweeping all sorts of debris beside leaves from sidewalks, driveways, and porches. As I got closer, I noticed her walkway wasn't all that much in need of sweeping. There was a scattering of leaves, a few twigs, and some stray grass clippings. That was good. She was probably just sweeping to kill time, which would mean she'd be happy to take a break from that chore and let me interview her.

"Hi, Mrs. Muscatello," I said, when I got close enough for her to hear me.

"Hello, Emma." She stopped sweeping.

I figured I'd get right to the point. That way, I wouldn't waste any time if she said no. "I need to interview someone for a school project. Are you busy? Can I ask you some questions?"

"You just did," she said.

I got it. That was a joke.

"Can I ask more questions?"

"It sure looks like you can," she said.

"Seriously . . . ," I paused, trying to figure out the best way to ask a question that didn't leave much room for smart answers.

"Of course you can ask me some questions." She pointed toward a pair of rocking chairs that stood side by side on her porch. "Let's go sit."

As we took our seats, she asked, "Is this for school?"

I wanted to say *No, it's my new hobby. I walk around doing interviews because it's more fun than collecting stamps or building models of famous ships.* But I didn't want to risk having her change her mind, so I just said, "Yeah. For language arts."

"When is it due?" she asked.

"You sound like my mom."

"I am a mom."

"Where are your kids?"

"Is this the interview, or the nosy neighbor?" she asked.

"Both, I guess." I opened my notebook and started writing as she answered my first question.

"My children are all grown up and have children of their own."

I asked more questions, and took notes. It was actually sort of fun. "Thank you so much," I said when I'd gotten enough material for my paper.

"You're welcome."

I closed my notebook, took out my phone, and snapped her picture.

"You should always ask permission first," she said.

The comment was so strange and unexpected, it took me a moment to realize she was talking about the photo. That was weird. Everyone was taking photos of everything all the time. "I'm sorry. I didn't know that. I need it for my paper. Do you want me to delete it?"

She shook her head. "I guess there's no harm. Good luck with your paper."

"Thanks." I headed home and got to work.

It took a little longer than I'd planned to turn my interview notes into an actual essay. Mom walked by my room at least once every five minutes, giving me those *I told you so* stares and sighing heavily enough to blow out all the candles on my grandfather's birthday cake. By the time I had the whole thing written, and added the photo from my phone, it was past my bedtime.

I sent my paper to the printer. I figured Mom was going to sigh even harder when I went downstairs to get it. But I was the one who ended up sighing. And maybe panicking, just a little. There was no essay in the output tray. Instead, there was a flashing light on the printer's control panel.

"Out of ink," I said as I read the error message. "No!" I slid open the desk drawer. It had at least ten or fifteen ink cartridges jammed inside. A quick search showed they were all empty.

I did my owl impression again as I looked around for help. *Who?* Drake was my best bet. I found him in the basement, playing *River Raid* on one of his antique game systems and eating popcorn.

"Can you help me print something?" I asked.

He sighed. But he followed me up to the living room and tapped the flashing light on the printer. "It can't print. It's out of ink."

"I *know* that," I said. "I figured you can do something. It can't be out of all the ink."

"You're right. Just one cartridge is dry. But it's impossible to print anything on this model printer when any of the colors runs out," he said.

"Then I'm out of luck," I said.

"No. You're in luck, because you have a brother who specializes in doing the impossible on a daily basis. Step aside, pathetic mortal."

I stepped aside. Drake opened the printer, fiddled with something, closed the printer, smirked, and said, "Try it now. There won't be any red, but it will still probably look okay."

It worked. I could hear the printer come alive, doing all the secret little things it had to do to make an image on paper. Drake returned to his dungeon stronghold. And Mrs. Muscatello emerged from the slot at the bottom of the printer, looking very blue and green. Because of that, and the fact that I was looking at the photo upside down, it took me a second to realize I was seeing something really strange.

I picked up the page and turned it around. Her body looked normal. But her head was so wrong, I couldn't accept what I was seeing. It just wasn't possible. I stared, trying to make the illusion go away. I held the photo at various angles. It remained what it was: A portrait of a fly. Mrs. Muscatello had the head of a fly! An enormous fly, with those bulging eyes and all that spikey fly hair whose name I can never remember, but I think it starts with an S or a C.

The image flickered. No. It was my hand that was shaking. I checked the photo on my phone. It was fine. I didn't know what to do. Tell my parents? What for? What would they do? Was there any reason to do anything? Maybe it was better if Mrs. Muscatello never knew I'd discovered her secret.

I decided I'd figure out what to do in the morning. But I couldn't sleep. I had to know more. After I heard my parents go to bed, I got up, threw on clothes, grabbed the photo, and slipped out the back door.

Mrs. Muscatello's house was dark. I didn't care. I knocked. And then, as I waited, and heard her footsteps approaching from inside, I forced myself not to run.

The door opened. "I suppose you want to talk," she said.

I nodded.

"Come in?"

I shook my head. There was no way I was stepping into that house. We took our seats on the porch.

"I guess you have more questions," she said.

I managed to nod and make a sound that somewhat resembled "Yes."

"I'm also guessing your printer ran out of a color," she said. "The protective coloration relies on the full visible spectrum."

"Red," I said. I swallowed, and then pushed out two more words. "Protective coloration?"

It was her turn to nod.

"What are you?"

"A person," she said.

The words escaped before I had a chance to think about them. "No, you aren't."

166

"That's not your decision," she said.

I kept my mouth shut and thought about that. *Person* had always seemed like an easy slot to fill. I was a person. So were my parents. Even Drake qualified, so the bar wasn't set very high. A rabbit wasn't a person. That was obvious. Neither was a horse. But we'd learned in school about how awful things could get when one group of people decided the members of another group weren't really people.

"You're right," I said. "It's not my decision."

"Thank you." She patted my leg.

I flinched, which made me feel guilty. "Sorry."

"I understand," she said. "Your reaction is as natural as my camouflage."

"I can get over it," I said.

"That's part of what makes us human," she said. "We can be better than we're designed to be. We can transcend our programming."

After another silence, she asked me, "Is my secret safe with you."

"Yeah." I thought about the way people react to insects. Some of us flinch. Some of us kill them on sight. A few of us study them in fascination, seeing beauty in their form. I handed her the picture. "Your secret's safe. I'll print another picture in the library, before class."

She thanked me again, and reached out to pat my leg. But she hesitated.

"It's okay," I said.

This time, I didn't flinch.

WATCH YOUR GRAMMAR

rom the Minutes of the Schranski School District Monthly Meeting, June of this year:

Edward Upton, head of the Schranski Middle School English Department has submitted a proposal for the district to purchase Kenyosa Corporation's Grammar Watches for the entire student population. In response to questioning, he explained: "Grammar Watches contain intelligent software that functions like a spell checker, but also uses speech recognition. If the watch detects a grammatical error, it issues a gentle reminder in the form of a low-voltage electrical shock. It's really just a small tingle. Studies show it improves student grammar by as much as seventy-three percent."

The board voted unanimously to create a committee to investigate the feasibility of purchasing Grammar Watches. Mr. Upton offered to write a grant application to obtain state and federal aid to help fund the project. The board approved this offer.

From the Minutes of the Schranski School District Monthly Meeting, *July of this year:*

The Grammar Watch committee reported that their research indicated the product would have a major positive impact on both student behavior and test results. Mr. Upton disclosed that he had received grants to cover eighty-five percent of the cost of acquiring a Grammar Watch for each student. The board voted unanimously to approve the project and provide funds for the remaining fifteen percent of the cost.

From the Minutes of the Schranski School District Monthly Meeting, *August of this year:*

The Grammar Watch committee reported that Grammar Watches have been obtained and will be distributed to each student on the first day of school, September 4th.

From the Minutes of the Schranski School District Monthly Meeting, *September of this year:*

The Grammar Watch committee reported that the Grammar Watch distribution has been achieved.

From the Minutes of the Schranski School District Monthly Meeting, *October of this year:*

Schranski Middle School principal Ethel Membaum advised the board that several parents were concerned when they discovered the Grammar Watches were not removable.

Schranski Middle School English Department head Edward Upton offered to write a memo for distribution to all middle school parents, explaining the need for this feature.

From the Minutes of the *Schranski School District Monthly Meeting, November of this year:*
Department heads for English, History, and Science reported that the students seemed unusually quiet this year.

Schranski Middle School debate team coach Salvador Biberoni reported to the board that the debate team has been disbanded, due to a lack of participation.

Mr. Lazlo Cuthbert, a representative of Kenyosa Corporation, provided the board with a presentation on available software upgrades for Grammar Watches. The board appointed a committee to investigate the offerings.

From the Minutes of the *Schranski School District Monthly Meeting, December of this year:*
A study on noise in the workplace revealed that the Schranski Middle School cafeteria was the quietest school cafeteria in the state.

Schranski Middle School announced a record low in teacher sick days.

The Upgrade Committee presented their findings and recommended a purchase of Grammar Watch foreign-language modules for all languages taught at Schranski Middle School. The board approved the purchase.

Students at Schranski Middle School submitted paperwork

requesting the formation of a Mime club. No students attended the meeting to speak about this request.

From the Minutes of the Schranski School District Monthly Meeting, January of this year:
Schranski Middle School music teacher, Dr. Lois Galante, reported to the board that the winter musical, *My Fair Lady*, about a professor who tries to teach a Cockney maid to speak proper English, was cancelled after nobody auditioned for the lead female role of Eliza Doolittle.

From the Minutes of the Schranski School District Monthly Meeting, February of this year:
Schranski Middle School Spanish teacher, Mr. Anthony Vega, reported that the Spanish Club, for which he is the advisor, has been disbanded, due to lack of attendance. French, Italian, and German club advisors gave similar reports.

Chess Club advisor, Ms. Dianna Ghupta, requested funds to purchase additional chess sets to meet the club's swelling membership.

From the Minutes of the Schranski School District Monthly Meeting, March of this year:
Schranski Middle School principal Ethel Membaum presented the results of the latest teacher-observation period. All monitors reported that they had never seen such well-behaved students. In virtually every classroom, not a single student

spoke out of turn or interrupted the teacher. The only negative finding was a drastic decline in class participation.

From the Minutes of the Schranski School District Monthly *Meeting, April of this year:*
Schranski Middle School band director, Mr. Elbert Simmons, reported that the spring musical, *Porgy and Bess,* was cancelled when students refused to sing "It Ain't Necessarily So."

From the Minutes of the Schranski School District Monthly *Meeting, May of this year:*
County Commissioner Ms. Wendy Probald provided the board with preliminary census data concerning new residents. Student population rose a typical five percent at all schools and in all grade levels, except for Schranski Middle School, where the student population in all grades combined declined by an unprecedented fourteen percent. Ms. Probald said the county was unable to explain the drop, and they believed it was just a statistical anomaly.

From the Minutes of the Schranski School District Monthly *Meeting, June of this year:*
Due to the overwhelming success of the Grammar Watch trial run, Coach Gus Miklaski, head of the Schranski Middle School Physical Education Department, has submitted a proposal for the district to purchase Kenyosa Corporation's Posture Belts.

Dr. Leonard Franklin, head of Schranski Middle School's Guidance Department, has submitted a proposal for the district to purchase Kenyosa Corporation's Positive Thinking Helmets.

Ms. Stella Munroe, head of Schranski Middle School's Reading Department, has submitted a proposal for the district to purchase Kenyosa Corporation's Anti-skimming Reading Glasses.

The board has appointed committees to investigate these suggestions.

AT STAKE

As the flames lick at my toes, all I can think about is how easily this could have been avoided. If only I hadn't opened my mouth. If only I hadn't spoken those two words that started me down the path to this horrible ending. And now, there's no one to hear me speak.

I'd been sitting in geography class, getting more and more annoyed as Mr. Ledona explained our next assignment. "I can't believe this," I whispered to Carl. "Is he crazy?"

Carl shook his head. "This is wrong. He's acting like we're college students or something. Nobody can write a twenty-five-page report. He's got to be out of his mind."

In the front of the room, Mr. Ledona kept on talking, telling us all the ugly details of our assignment. "I'll expect each of you to use at least ten different sources. Legitimate sources. Not some unreliable internet site."

"How about ten identical sources?" I whispered to Carl. "I can manage that."

Carl frowned as he tried to digest this. "But they'd all be the same," he said. He doesn't always get what I mean right away. If ever.

"That was a joke," I said.

"Oh." His frown deepened, but then he nodded. "I get it."

"I'll also require a properly formatted bibliography, of course," Mr. Ledona said. "You'll follow the guidelines described in the *Chicago Manual of Style*."

The murmuring increased. Mr. Ledona didn't seem to notice. Or maybe he enjoyed piling us up with impossible tasks.

"I'm not doing it," I told Carl.

"You'll flunk," Carl said.

"I don't care." I glared at the teacher

"One more thing," Mr. Ledona said. "I expect each report to have footnotes and an index."

Something inside me just snapped. "Drop dead," I muttered. But it came out louder than a mutter. It came out loud enough for the back half of the room to hear me.

Half the heads in the classroom turned toward me.

At exactly the same time, the rest of the heads were staring at the front of the room, where Mr. Ledona let out a gasp as he slumped to the ground.

A couple kids raced up to him. I sat there, gripping my desk.

"He's dead," someone said.

"No way." I stood up and tried to look past the growing crowd for signs of life in the crumpled body on the floor.

Everything happened real quickly after that. Paramedics came. They raced out with Mr. Ledona on a gurney. But by then, even from far away, he didn't look like a living person.

We were left standing in the aisles or sitting at our desks, a class without a teacher.

"You killed him," someone said.

I looked toward my accuser. It was Rochelle Bebstock, that self-righteous mean girl who always found fault in others.

"Murderer," Danny Hamilton said. He had a crush on Rochelle, and would do anything to impress her.

Everyone was staring at me. I was used to that. They stared at me all the time, just because I didn't play their stupid games, or wear the clothes they wore, or get the latest trendy haircut. But this was different. I shifted my eyes from face to face.

There was no sign of their usual sneers of superiority. They all looked scared and angry. That's a bad combination.

"Boo!" I shouted.

They jumped back. I started laughing. I suspect that might have been a mistake.

"Freak." Dexter Thorp walked up to me and raised a fist. I guess I should have been careful around him, because he's big, mean, and stupid—another bad combination. But I wasn't afraid. I'd been beaten up before. Besides, right now, I felt invulnerable.

"Go ahead," I said. "Hit me. See what happens." I stared right at him. I wasn't scared. But Dexter was. I could tell.

Dexter backed away from me. "It wouldn't be worth the suspension."

The bell rang and we spread out to other classrooms throughout the school. The rumor must have spread, too. As the day wore on, more and more whispers and stares followed me through the halls.

I felt sort of bad for Mr. Ledona. He wasn't any worse than my other teachers, except for that term paper thing, which I guess wasn't a problem anymore. But I didn't feel guilty. That would have been ridiculous. Because it wasn't my fault. He probably had clogged arteries or something. I'd bet he ate the wrong stuff and never bothered to get any exercise. I wasn't going to feel guilty over a stupid coincidence.

I had to walk past Dexter and his buddies on the way out of school. Normally I would have ignored them, or waited until they left, but this time I stared at them, smiling the whole time, like I knew a dark and dangerous secret. Dexter stared back. But I noticed a couple of the others wouldn't look at me. Cool. School was going to be a lot more fun for the rest of the year.

I turned on my music and headed home. After dinner I went outside, to eliminate the impossible thought that had been nagging at my mind. There's a maple tree near the edge of the backyard. As I expected, I saw a squirrel in one of the branches.

"Drop dead," I said, staring straight at it.

It stared back, then ran off, not the least bit dead. Another squirrel ran past me on the ground. I tried to remember how my voice had sounded that morning. And how I had felt. And, even more so, how much I wanted the words to come true.

"Drop dead."

It dropped.

I was surprised. But not totally. I'd always suspected I was special. That's why I didn't fit in. That's why all the stupid stuff the others cared about never interested me. I knelt by the body of the squirrel. "Live." No response. I tried a couple other ways to reverse what I'd done. No luck. Hate came much more easily to me than love. It looked like this was a one-way trick. That's okay. I wasn't planning to kill anyone I'd want to revive.

I had dinner in my room. My parents know enough to leave me alone when I'm in there. I had some heavy thinking to do. Being able to kill gave me an awesome power. But I needed to figure out the best way to use that ability.

Even an idiot could see lots of ways I could exploit my gift. From now on, I could get what I wanted by using fear as my weapon. That's how things would go at school. If people knew, or even suspected, that I could turn them into cold, lifeless slabs of protein, they'd do anything I asked. But fear meant danger. We destroy the things we fear, if we get the chance. I'd have to watch my back.

There had to be better ways to use my power than just scaring students and teachers. I could kill people and rob them. That would be easy. I'd only do it to bad people, of course. Criminals. Yeah. That would work. Maybe. Still, I'd have to be careful. I'm not sure how I'd get them alone. It's not like I wanted to kill a bunch of people at once. I'm not a monster.

Though that could be sort of cool. I smiled as I pictured a cluster of bad guys dropping dead, crumpling to the ground at the same time.

Yeah. That would be slick. I could be an army of one. For the highest bidder, of course.

My phone rang, dissolving the fantasy image.

"Yeah?"

It was Carl. "Want to make some money?" His voice was quivering.

"Sure. How?"

"I'd rather tell you in person."

"Okay. Where?"

"How about the park?" he asked.

"Pritchard's Park?"

"No. The one behind my place."

"Got it. I'll head out, now."

"See ya."

I was pretty sure I knew what he wanted. He lived with his uncle, and the guy was really mean. Carl wanted me to kill him.

My first job, I thought. My first good job, that is. I'd had a couple low-paying summer jobs. Which led to a very important question: How much should I ask?

I guess it depended on how much he had. It's not like I could tell him I wanted a thousand bucks if he only had a couple hundred. Of course, he could sell his uncle's stuff. Or I could even ask for some of the stuff. No. I didn't want to start trading death for silverware and stereo speakers, or try to figure out how to sell my loot without raising suspicion.

When I reached the edge of the park, I looked around for Carl. There was nobody in sight.

"Over here," Carl whispered.

I spotted him just inside a dense cluster of trees. "What's the big secret?" I asked. I knew why he'd called me, but I wanted to make him say it.

"Can you really kill people?" he asked.

"Yeah."

"For sure?" He edged a step back, as if he suddenly wondered whether he was at risk.

"Definitely." I stepped closer. "Want a demonstration?"

He stared at me, once again lagging in his ability to get what I meant. Finally, he screamed "No!" and threw up his hands in front of his face, as if that could stop my power.

"Just kidding." I let out a laugh.

"I knew that." But he backed away a bit more, and his eyes shifted past me.

That's when I got grabbed from behind. Someone pinned my arms to my sides. Someone else tied a rag around my face, pulling it tight against my mouth like a gag. I tried to shout, but couldn't form any words.

A couple seconds more, and my hands were tied behind my back. I glared at Carl. "Drop dead!"

Thanks to the gag, my shout was a muffled cry. I had no power. Carl kept breathing.

"Witch!"

The speaker spun me around. Rochelle.

"Demon," Danny said, stepping up next to her.

There were others in the group. About ten, in all. Not that the number mattered, now that I was tied up. They dragged me deeper into the woods.

When they stopped walking, my own heart almost stopped beating.

The scene in front of me looked like the set from one of those medieval witch trial movies. A stake—actually, a fence post—had been stuck in the ground. The soil looked freshly dug. There was kindling around the post, and larger branches piled on top of that.

My knees buckled as I realized what they were planning to do.

"No!"

I struggled, but they dragged me to the post and tied me there. I glared at Carl. He shrugged, as if he hadn't realized it would go this far, but wasn't all that upset now that it had.

"Die, witch," Danny said. He knelt and lit the kindling. The flames licked at my toes.

As I'd said, all of this could have been avoided, if only I'd kept my mouth shut.

It was too late for that, now. I screamed and jerked against the ropes. They held. As I struggled, thrashed, and yelled, the gag moved just the tiniest bit. I could feel it pull down a little. But not enough to come free. It was caught across my nose. I shouted again, moving my jaw violently, pretending to be terrified while I tried to work the gag off my mouth. It wasn't hard to pretend. I was scared. But, more than that, I was angry.

I felt a sharp pain on my lower legs as the flames rose. I had to hurry.

"Witch!" Rochelle called again. As if the flames weren't enough, she lifted a rock and hurled it at me.

Her aim was terrible. The rock was going to go wide. But I leaned toward it, as much as the ropes would allow, and let it hit me right in the face.

I felt the worst pain I'd ever experienced as the rock crushed my nose.

Perfect.

I bent my head and jammed my chin against my chest as high up as I could, trapping the gag. Then I pushed my head forward, dragging my chin against my chest, tugging down on the cloth.

Agony.

The gag slipped down a little.

I repeated the motion, like an infant struggling to kick off a heavy comforter.

My nose and legs both felt on fire.

But the gag finally freed itself from my crushed nose and fell from my face. My mouth was no longer bound.

I was so furious, rage clouded reason. "DROP DEAD!" I howled at them.

At all of them.

They all dropped. Except for Carl. Somehow, he was still on his feet. He could free me. I looked him in the eye, hoping to see some sign of mercy.

But I saw no sign of anything. His eyes were empty. He was dead, too. He'd just lagged a bit behind everyone else, for one last time. As I realized this, he fell forward, joining the rest of the slain scattered across the forest floor.

They were sprawled on the ground in front of me, as life-less as Mr. Ledona or the squirrel. I'd killed all of them. Nobody was left to set me free. Nobody was left to put an end to this.

That would be the fire's job.

RUMPLECODESPIN

Once upon a time, there lived a young girl who wasn't very good about getting her homework done on time. So, one evening on a school night, she sat in her room, staring at her keyboard as the last hour shrank rapidly toward the last minute.

"I'm doomed," she whispered. She started to cry.

"What's wrong?" a strange little man asked. He was standing just outside her doorway, thin as a stray cat, dressed in rumpled jeans and a rumpled black T-shirt. Even seated at her desk, she was taller than him, so she didn't feel any fear.

"I'm supposed to code a video game for school," she said. "But I sort of waited too long. And now, I'm going to fail." As she said *fail*, she added a poetic wail and flopped her head into her waiting hands.

The strange little man—let's call him SLM—thumped his chest and said, "Your worries are over. I can spin out streams of code in the blink of an eye."

"You can?" she asked, as a glimmer of hope grew in her heart.

"Certainly," he said. "I was born to code."

"Will you code a game for me?" she asked.

"That depends," he said. "What will you give me in return?"

She scanned her room, searching for something she wouldn't miss, and spotted a watch she never wore. She dangled it in front of him. "How about this?"

"Deal," the man said. "Step aside."

He shooed her out of her chair, took a seat, and tapped the keys so fast his fingers blurred. She watched the screen as the lines scrolled past, amazed at the way SLM spun out a slew of code.

"Done," he said a few minutes later.

The girl gasped. On the screen she saw a perfectly adequate video game involving colorful pieces of fruit and a slingshot. When she handed over the watch, she promised herself she'd be more diligent next time, and not wait until the last minute to do her assignments.

But she wasn't. Barely a month later, as she wailed and wept and glared at her keyboard, SLM returned. This time, she needed to create a useful app for keeping track of her books, magazines, sports equipment, or some other collection. And this time, SLM took a necklace she no longer wore in exchange for spinning out code.

As SLM departed, the girl promised herself she'd absolutely, definitely, positively be more diligent in the future.

She was true to her word, for a month and a half. And then, she wasn't. Ten minutes before bedtime, she still didn't have an app that could create cryptogram puzzles. That's when SLM appeared.

But this time, nothing in her room interested him, though

she was desperate enough to offer him even objects she knew she'd miss.

Finally, he said, "I will do it, but if you ever become a pet owner, you must give me your first pet."

"Deal," the girl said, as a surge of relief pulled her out of despair. That was a safe offer for her to accept. She was petless, and fairly sure her parents planned for her to remain so.

She'd totally forgotten about the whole thing a year later, when her dad surprised her with the cutest Poodle-Beagle-Dachshund puppy she'd ever seen.

SLM came back that night. "I'm here for your first pet," he said. "I've always wanted a Poobeadash."

"No," she screamed. "Take anything else. Take *everything* else." She grabbed a handful of rings and necklaces from her jewelry chest and thrust them at him.

"Sorry. We have a deal. But to show you I have a heart, I will make you an offer. If you can guess my name within three days, you can keep your dog." He laughed, like this was an impossible task.

"Really?" she asked.

"Really and truly," he said. "But you never will."

When SLM came back the next day, the girl, who had put off thinking about the problem until the last minute, spewed out a series of wild guesses.

"Rufus?" she said. He looked like a *Rufus*.

"No."

"Tyberius?"

"Nope."

"Sarsaparilla?"

"Now you're just wasting my time," he said.

The next night, things didn't go much better. He wasn't Aaron, Abner, Ace, Adonis, Aegis, Afton, or any of the other guesses she'd methodically listed, having actually put a bit of thought into the problem.

"How about my phone?" she asked, holding it up like it was a precious jewel. "Will you take that, instead?"

"Not a chance," he said. "I want the dog. And he'll be all mine, tomorrow."

On the third and final night, the girl tried again, making more bad guesses, like Zoopy, Contripunto, Clamface, and Moxflox. She knew those were ridiculous attempts. She was just doing this to give SLM the feeling he'd won, and to make her last-second victory feel all that much sweeter. This time, she was prepared.

"Hand over the puppy," SLM said when the girl had finished her list.

"Not quite yet," she said. "I have one more name to guess."

"It won't help," SLM said.

"I think it will," she said. "I took your photo, yesterday."

"Wonderful. You'll have something to remember me by as you weep at the loss of your pet," he said. "Now hand over that puppy."

"Not so fast, Rumplecodespin," she said.

He let out a gasp. "No! You couldn't have!"

She let out a laugh as his expression told her she had won.

"How did you know?" the man screeched.

"Easy," she said. "Hardly anyone can resist posting selfies. That's why I took your photo last time. I did an image search. And there you were, all over the internet. You really do like to brag about what a great coder you are."

The man let out a howl that was louder than his gasp and

screech combined, and stomped his foot so hard it broke through the floor. That made him even angrier. He tried to run off. Which was not a great idea since his foot was stuck. He pulled a groin muscle pretty badly before he freed himself from the hole.

And then he hobbled off, gasping in pain with each agonizing step.

The girl hugged her puppy and promised herself she'd be more diligent with her homework from now on, and ever after.

And she was.

For at least a month or two.

I CAN'T QUITE PUT
A FINGER ON IT

It took me a moment to realize what I was seeing. That's how strange it was. But when it sunk in, I couldn't keep from blurting out my reaction.

"Your finger!" I shouted, pointing at Ridley Iverson's left hand, where it rested on his desk.

Up front, Mr. Pierson shot me a glare. I clamped my mouth shut, but turned my attention back to Ridley. His little finger was gone, as if removed by a highly skilled surgeon. Or a magician.

Ridley frowned, like he had no idea what I was talking about. My face grew warm when I realized that, whatever had happened to him, he didn't want to talk about it. And he certainly didn't want me to point it out. I'd been a jerk.

But when we got up to go to lunch, he said, "What was that about?"

Now, I felt even more embarrassed. "I was wondering what happened. . . ." I didn't even dare point. I just nodded in the direction of his hand. "You know . . ."

"No, I don't know," he said.

I guess he was going to make me suffer a bit. "Your hand," I said. "Your little finger."

He held up his right hand and wiggled the little finger. "What about it?"

I shoved my own hands in my pockets and tried to think of a way out of this. I came up empty. It looked like I'd have to answer his question. "No, not that one. The other one."

Ridley stared down at his left hand and frowned. "I have no idea what you're talking about."

Now I really wished I'd kept my mouth shut in the first place. "Your little finger," I said. "It's gone. Something happened to it."

"I've never had one," he said. "You have a really wild imagination." He walked off, leaving me staring at his back.

Never had one?

I thought back. Every image I had of Ridley included that little finger. But I couldn't help doubting my memories. That doubt vanished the next Friday morning, exactly one week later, when I took my seat. Ridley's left ring finger was gone.

It was brutal keeping my mouth shut. But I couldn't think of any way to ask him about it. Really, what could I say? *Hey, Ridley, didn't you use to have a ring finger?*

The whole day, I kept sneaking glances at it, trying to spot any sort of clue about what could steal away both a finger and the memory of once having it. There was no explanation. There was just a deep-seated feeling that something was very wrong with the world. Or, at least, with Ridley's world. And mine as well, I guess, since I was observing this wrongness.

The next week, when his middle finger had joined the ranks of the missing, I decided I had to find out what was happening. I waited until Thursday before I put my plan in action.

Ridley lived just a few blocks away from me, in a new development. There was a half-finished house on the lot right behind him. I went there after school. I know it's trespassing to go into one of those places, but my curiosity was far stronger than my fear of getting in trouble. I discovered that there was a window on the second floor that gave me a good view of Ridley's kitchen. I spotted him at the table. Even from this distance, I could see his left hand still had one finger and a thumb. My stomach lurched as my brain seized on the question of where all of this would end. Would it stop after he'd lost all the fingers on that hand? After he'd lost all ten of his fingers? All his fingers and toes? All his limbs?

I forced myself to quit thinking about that part, but decided I'd have to sneak out of my house and return here at night so I could spy on Ridley while he slept. For some reason, maybe because he was unaware of the change, I figured that whatever was going on, it must have happened while he was asleep. Besides, it just didn't seem like something that could happen while the sun was shining.

It turned out I was somewhat right about that. And somewhat wrong. As I discovered when I watched him from my hiding spot in the unfinished house, his hand hadn't changed, yet. His bedroom was directly above the kitchen. I'd brought binoculars, which I thought was also probably a crime. I didn't care. They allowed me to see a magnified view of Ridley asleep in his bed, and catch a glimpse of his hand. It was still as intact as it had been that morning.

I hoped something would happen soon. I wasn't eager to spend all night spying on him. I lowered the binoculars so I could shift into a more comfortable position. That's when a motion on Ridley's roof caught my eye. Something half the size of a man slithered, snakelike, down the roof. It disappeared beneath the eaves. I guess it had squeezed into the attic. I didn't see whether it entered Ridley's room through the door or a vent. Either way, once it was inside, it approached his bed.

My horror grew as the creature grabbed him by the hair and flung him against the wall. At that point, he was no longer asleep. He lay there, crumpled, screaming so loudly I could hear his cries through his closed window. His bedroom door flew open. As his parents raced in, I braced myself for a scene of slaughter. But the creature turned his head in their direction and leaped directly in front of them, so close they must have felt its foul breath. Instead of flinching, they froze, as if time had stopped. The monster pressed his forehead against each of theirs, mother first, and then father. Their faces grew slack, losing all signs of fear. They left the room, walking away as if nothing was wrong.

The monster turned its attention back to Ridley. It seized his left arm and raised the hand to its mouth. I don't need to describe the rest. It was awful. Throughout this brutal feeding, Ridley howled with a mix of terror and pain that nearly turned my bowels to water.

And then, the creature shoved its face forward, pressing its forehead against Ridley's. His own face grew slack. The creature wiped away Ridley's tears and put him back in bed. I watched it step out of view, and then reappear beneath the eaves.

As it made its way to the roof, I drew in a gasping breath. The creature froze in the middle of its climb, then turned its head in my direction. I ducked beneath the windowsill. When I peeked out a moment later, it was gone. I was relieved it hadn't spotted me.

My relief didn't last long. The first scratch of claws against the outside wall of the house shot me to my feet. I raced down the steps and out through the front doorway, cutting across the unfinished yards of unfinished houses, running faster than I'd ever run in my life. I didn't even risk looking over my shoulder until I reached my block.

I didn't see the monster behind me. I'd escaped. I knew what I'd seen would haunt me forever, but at least I hadn't been caught. It was hours before I finally managed to fall asleep. And after that, I know I slept poorly. I had a hard time waking up for school, and still felt half asleep when I got there and took my seat at my desk.

That's weird. I looked at Ridley's left hand where it rested on his desk. All it had was a thumb. No fingers. I wanted to ask him about it, but that would have been rude. I checked my own hands, as if to reassure myself they were intact.

Yup. They were just the way they'd always been, with a thumb and four fingers on my right hand, and a thumb and three fingers on my left.

A WORD OR TWO ABOUT THESE STORIES

As always, here's a look behind the scenes at the various sparks of inspiration that led to these stories.

How to Slay Vampires for Fun and Profit
One of my main sources for ideas is my "what if" file. Every morning, my first writing task is to think up one "what if" question and write it down. The file has reached eighty pages. This story came from that file. I wasn't very specific when I wrote the idea. It was basically just, "What if vampires tricked people into thinking they were going to trap them?" The idea of a "how to" book in a library came to me when I was trying to figure out the best way to turn the idea into a story.

Come Back Soon
I've written a lot of time travel stories, including a funny one, "Frozen in Time," where a girl keeps answering the door to find her older self, who has come back in time to issue a warning, and a wonderfully icky story, "Two Timers," which involves traveling in two directions at once. As you might suspect, this is not an advisable journey. (Both stories

can be found in *Strikeout of the Bleacher Weenies*.) In the current case, the spark was "what if you could travel back in time, but only a minute or two?" I shortened the time to meet the needs of the plot.

All that Glitters

Sometimes, I'll try to get ideas for these collections by thinking about what sort of monsters I've been overlooking. (The first Weenies book, *In the Land of the Lawn Weenies*, had a lot of monster stories. As I worked on subsequent books, the mix shifted to a much broader spectrum of fiction, but I like to make sure there are enough monster stories in each collection to please those readers who love that particular subgenre.) Weenies fans know there is no shortage of vampires in these pages, and witches seem to show up fairly regularly. But I realized I've only written two or three werewolf stories, so I started thinking about them, which led me to the transmutation idea.

Bald Truths

There are stories in the news fairly regularly about people who shave their heads to support someone who is undergoing chemotherapy. As I thought about that, I decided I wanted the inevitable bullies who mock such people to suffer a horrible fate. It took a little work to make that happen, but I feel it was worth it.

Tough Crowd

Since I love comedy and jokes so much, it's not surprising I had an idea about a kid who has to make someone laugh every day. (The "have to do X every day" theme is fairly common in fantasy stories.) I guess I love chocolate, too. But that's another story.

Gordie's Gonna Git Ya

This one made quite a journey. My original idea was, "What if a kid went to a new school and was immediately popular?" That's not a bad idea, by itself. Especially if the kid wasn't popular at his old school. I knew it would be fun to write. (Scenes that conflict with the main character's expectations are always fun for me. And if something is fun for me, there's a good chance it will also be fun for the reader.) But the real question is: What caused this popularity? As I was thinking about that, the idea of an urban legend came to mind. And that led me to Gordie.

Fairyland

This started with the amusing question, "What if kids traveled to fairyland, and it turned out to be a wretched place?" I had a lot of fun making the place as horrible as possible. I think, in my mind, the twins might have spoken in fake British accents, but I couldn't find the right place to slip that information into the narrative, so I didn't put that in the story.

Off the Beaten Track

This story was inspired by a classic puzzle about how to escape an oncoming train. The trick with the puzzle is that it is set up so if you try to run away, you'll never make it. So you have to go against your instincts and run toward the train. (I used the same concept in one of the video games I designed, *Frogger II*, for the GameBoy. There's a level where you have to get past large rolling fireballs. At one point, if you run away, you'll never make it.) I'm always a bit apprehensive when I use a story with a real-life monster rather than an imaginary creature. But I think my readers can handle this one.

The Sword in the Stew

Beside my "what if?" file, I also like to write lists of titles, hoping one of them will inspire a story. And one of my favorite types of titles are those that play with well-known fables, classic stories, or fairy tales. In this case, *The Sword in the Stone*, which is the title of a classic book about King Arthur, led me to "The Sword in the Stew."

The Doll Collector

Dolls can be pretty creepy. Doll heads can be even creepier. I started by wondering, "What if a girl visited a relative who had a collection of doll heads?" In the first draft of the story, I had one of the heads roll off the shelf and try to bite the lamp cord to make the room dark. That seemed like a good idea. But as I was revising the story, I spotted a flaw in my logic. (Note that fantasy is not exempt from logic. You can have amazing things happen, but they still have to make sense within the rules of the story's magic.) If a doll head could roll off the shelf, why did all the others have to settle for inching themselves forward by chomping? It didn't make sense. So I changed it. And, as often happens, the new scene, with her flinging the head across the room, was more powerful than the original one. (This is yet another reason why I love revision.)

Physics for Toons

This started as, "What if the real world had the same physics as cartoons?" From there, I could have gone in a lot of directions. I had the story mostly written a while ago, but I couldn't come up with a satisfying ending after the part where the TV went blank. Eventually, I revisited it, and the idea of the narrator putting his head on backwards hit me. I knew that was the way to go, and that the scene would be pure joy to write.

The Heart of a Dragon

Sometimes, I'll just start writing. That's what I did here. I felt in the mood to have some characters snatched by a dragon. A while back, I wrote a much more light-hearted dragon story, "Dragon Around," which also started by my writing a snatched-by-a-dragon scene. That one can be found in *Attack of the Vampire Weenies*. But this one felt like it had to be dark.

Searching for a Fart of Gold

Yeah, I actually wondered what would happen if you could fart gold. I was working on two different gold stories at the time. The other one, where a kid's fingers start to turn into gold after he picks goldenrod, just wasn't working, even though I had an ending in mind, so I set it aside. At first, I had no idea how to end this one, either. As you can see, I finally figured things out. (By the way, while I often begin writing without knowing how I'll end a story, don't take that as the best process for everyone. When you're learning how to write fiction, it's a good idea to have the ending in mind. And the middle. But the more writing you do, the more you can take a leap of faith at the start of the journey, and assume you'll probably be able to pull some sort of rabbit out of some sort of hat at the end.)

On One Condition

I had very good science classes when I went to high school. In biology, the teacher told us about conditioning and revealed that she and her classmates once managed to get a professor to keep his hand on his chin when he lectured the class. You can get a lot of great ideas for stories by thinking about things you learned or things that happened to you in school.

Ghost Dancer

I like to think about urban myths. There are all sorts of stories about ghostly brides or other people who haunt some event on a regular basis. But I also like kids who love science. And I know that school dances can be difficult for lots of kids. So I put all of that together. In the original idea, it was the main character who was going to be the ghost. But I realized it would be more fun for her to help a friend. I also had a serious issue to deal with. The whole idea that girls have to sit around and wait for an invitation to dance is very old-fashioned. I was worried I'd get criticized for writing a story where that happened. But traditions change slowly, and I think it's fine to write a story like this as long as I make it clear that things are changing. (By the way, if you love seeing kids use science to solve problems, check out my series: *Nathan Abercrombie, Accidental Zombie*. In the second book, *Dead Guy Spy*, Nathan's science genius friend, Abigail, figures out how to help him get through his doctor's exam even though he doesn't have a heart beat or a normal body temperature.)

Check out the Library Weenies

I wanted to make the title of this book very special. There have been all sorts of Weenies, but I think this might be the last or next to last collection. I made all sorts of lists, trying to think of the perfect candidate. One of the titles I wrote was *Library Weenies*. (The "Check Out" part came later.) As much as I liked that idea, I was worried about going against a structure I'd established. For the first eight books, the Weenies were someone mockable, like those joggers who never smiled, or the people who loved their lawns a little too much. In the case of Library Weenies, the Weenies would be the good guys. But I trusted my readers to understand this. I did ask some book sellers and librarians what they thought of the title. Dave Richardson of Blue Marble Books in Fort Thomas, Kentucky, who has always been a strong supporter of my books, responded by telling me, "That's your opening sentence." And he was right. It's a great way to start the story. That helped lead me to the rest of the tale.

Call Me
When I got my first smart phone, I thought about calling myself. I never bothered, and I still don't know what would happen. But I did hang on to the idea and jot it down. Speaking of which—always write down your ideas as soon as they hit you. Otherwise, they can easily vanish. And that would be tragic.

The Running of the Hounds
Often, before doing any writing, I will start my working day by reading something. When I'm writing these stories, I like to read about monsters, myths, unsolved mysteries, and legends. I stumbled across a mention of Gabriel Ratchets in a book called *Monsters Who's Who*, and knew I wanted to put them in a story. Originally, I had a different story in the collection,

inspired by the entry in that same book about Banshees, but it still needed work, so I replaced it with this one. (Stories get pulled or added to the manuscript up to the last minute, as my editor and I try to make the collection as strong as possible.) By the way, Gabriel Hounds have nothing to do with the angel by that name, and ratchets are dogs that hunt by scent. In some versions of the legend, they are actually geese. Legends are funny, that way.

A Boy and His Frog

When my daughter was little, she won a goldfish at a carnival. I didn't expect it to live long. It surprised me. It lived for many years, and never stopped growing. One year, we pet-sat a neighbor's son's frog while they went on vacation. I guess those two things combined to put the idea in my mind of a frog that never stopped growing.

Black Friday

As you can see from the first story, I'm always looking for interesting places and ways for vampires to hunt. And I'm always amazed at the frenzy of shopping that happens on Black Friday. Again, two things melded together nicely to give me one idea. You can get endless story ideas by combining two concepts. One of my most popular novels, *Hidden Talents*, happened because I thought up a way to combine misbehavior with something completely unexpected.

Romeo, Romeo, Wherefloor Argle Roblio?

This started with, "What if kids used infinite monkeys to write their essays?" That idea raises an interesting question. If you actually did have infinite monkeys typing away, is it possible that they could produce anything that ever was or would be written? But I'm not sure that means any specific thing would necessarily be created. In other words, they could write *Hamlet*, but that doesn't mean they would inevitably have to write *Hamlet*, even if given infinite time. I could be wrong about this. Infinity is as tricky to think about as time travel. I do know, given infinite time, or even a decent span of finite time, I'd personally much rather write new stories.

My Family History
When I visit schools, I often see assignments on display in the hallways. That got me thinking about how an assignment could be used to lure someone into a trap. This was actually a pretty tricky story to write, because the teacher had to care enough to want to visit the home, but if I made her too nice, people would hate the ending.

When Death Comes Calling
My original idea was, "What if a kid helped out Death?" I was thinking in terms of a summer job. But I decided it would be more interesting if the help was given unwittingly.

2D or Not 2D
Three-D is all the rage right now. Most blockbuster movies come with a three-D version, and three-D printers are popping up everywhere. It's always fun to take ideas or inventions and run them in the opposite direction. I actually combined this with another idea from my files, "What if insects from a book came to life?" When I was a kid, I was always sort of creeped out by the encyclopedia page that showed large drawings of various ants. I didn't mind ants, themselves, but

there was something creepy about the larger-than-life illustrations.

Mummy Misses You

This was another idea from my files, "What if a kid wrapped in bandages is mistake by a mummy for her son?" As with most ideas, this could have turned out a lot of different ways. It could have been scary. It could have been funny. It turned out sort of sad, which made me wonder whether to include it. I don't want anyone to feel sad. But I guess a sad story is okay once in a while, as long as it's surrounded by tales of farts, explosions, giant frogs, and thirsty vampires.

Seeing Red

This is a case where a simple life experience inspired a story. My color printer is always running out of ink at the worst time. When things like that happen, I tend to look at them in terms of plots.

Watch Your Grammar

One of the best parts about writing short-story collections is that I can try all sorts of things. I've written a story that consists of just one person talking ("Yackity-Yak" from *The Battle of the Red Hot Pepper Weenies*), and one that is nothing but dialogue. (That one, "M.U.B," for Monster Under the Bed, from *Wipeout of the Wireless Weenies*, has become my favorite one to read at schools. I'll pull a student from the audience and we'll read it together as a play.) I've written a story from the viewpoint of a baby and one about sentient sand. So I'm always looking for new things to try. I decided it would be fun to write a story using minutes from a school board meeting.

It's a bit subtler than some of my stories, and it's not a common format, so I hope you enjoyed it and appreciate the amazing variety of ways there are to tell a tale. (I think your parents might get a kick out of this one, if you show it to them. Especially if they go to school board meetings.)

At Stake

This story started when I was playing around by writing openings. I wasn't sure where it would go. And it ended up going in a very dark direction. It's another one where I wasn't sure whether it was too upsetting for younger readers. (If you like even darker stories, I've collected some of those in *Extremities: Stories of Death, Murder, and Revenge*.)

Rumplecodespin

Fairy tales make a great starting point for getting story ideas. You can play with the ideas, and ask things like, "What if sleeping beauty snored?" (I'll admit that's probably not going to lead to a story, but it was the first example that came to mind, and I think it's important to realize that not all ideas will work, but any idea can be a springboard to a better idea.) Or, as I mentioned when I wrote "The Sword in the Stew," you can play with a title, to see if that inspires an idea. That's what happened here. Thanks to that method, I've written "Little Bread Riding Hood," "The Princess and the Pea Brain," and several other stories for past Weenies collections.

I Can't Quite Put a Finger On It

Faithful Weenies fans know I put the scariest story last in each collection. I think this one is about as creepy as I'd want to go, and I know it's very dark. It started when I had the idea for a monster that can make its victims forget they've been victimized.

Well, that brings us to the end of another collection. If you've read all nine Weenies books, you've read three hundred short stories, written from 1994 through 2017. And if this is your first encounter with the Weenies, I hope the stories left you eager to seek out the other volumes. Either way, I feel fortunate that I'm able to share my love of short stories with an enthusiastic audience. And I'm thrilled that I've had the chance to explore a variety of styles, voices, viewpoints, sub-genres, and narrative structures as I told these tales. Whether you are a young reader, a teacher, a librarian, a parent, or a bookseller (or any combination of those things), I thank you for your part in all of this.

And now, because some stories aren't meant to be short, I invite you to turn to page 218 to enjoy a small sample of a new novel I am very excited about.

READING AND ACTIVITY GUIDE

Check Out the Library Weenies:
And Other Warped and Creepy Tales
Ages 9–12; Grades 4–7

ABOUT THIS GUIDE

The questions and activities that follow are intended to enhance your reading of *Check Out the Library Weenies*, the ninth book in David Lubar's popular anthology series. This guide has been developed in alignment with the Common Core State Standards. However please feel free to adapt this content to suit the needs and interests of your students or reading group participants.

WRITING AND RESEARCH ACTIVITIES

I. Short, But Not Always Sweet, Stories

A. David Lubar is a modern master of the short-story genre, especially tales that feature dark humor, twists and turns. Go to the library or online to develop a list of other authors of short stories or poems, from famous dark-tale teller Edgar Allan Poe to more contemporary writers. Select one author to research further. Use the information you gather to put together an oral presentation, describing the author's most famous, or popular, works, story inspirations, writing process, and some of the most common themes and literary devices that appear in the works. Present your findings to friends or classmates. In small groups, discuss the similarities and differences among the short-story authors covered in the presentations. As you're reading *Check Out the Library Weenies*, consider how the stories in this anthology follow, or break out of, patterns you identified in researching and discussing the short-story genre. (If you've read other Weenies anthologies, you might also consider how this volume is similar to, or different from, its predecessors.)

B. Many of the stories in *Check Out the Library Weenies* take unexpected twists and turns. There's usually a "tipping-point" moment, when things escalate into the story's core problem, or catastrophe. For example, the line from "Mummy Misses You": "The trouble began when we went to the Ancient Civilizations wing." As you read stories from this anthology, make a list of tipping, or turning, points. Think about the kind of language that "signals" this moment, or realization, for the main character. When you are done reading the stories and recording tipping points, review your list. Which tipping-point moment is (or moments are) the most effective, and why? Explain your answer in a short essay. Be sure to include relevant quotes and references from the stories to support your opinion.

II. **From Head to Tale: Bringing Your Wildest Themes to Life**

A. A special feature of David Lubar's Weenies anthologies is the story notes he includes, which offer readers (and aspiring writers) insights into his writing process and inspirations.

In his story notes for "Black Friday," David Lubar says, "You can get endless story ideas by combining two concepts." For example, he is intrigued by considering where vampires might hunt their human prey, as well as the cultural phenomenon of frenzied shopping on the Friday after Thanksgiving, which kicks off the holiday season in retail, but it is the *intersection* of those two ideas that drives the tale. Brainstorm a list of concepts that are of interest to you, then write a two to four-page short story that combines two of the ideas from your list. Consider making it a scary, or fantasy, story in keeping with the spirit of most of the stories in this collection.

B. David Lubar treats a wide range of subjects and themes in the *Check Out the Library Weenies* collection, including monsters, technology gone awry, time travel, unusual powers and opportunities, urban legends, and bullies, to name a few. Can you list some other themes David Lubar explores in this anthology? List each theme as a column head on a chart or spreadsheet. As you read, list each story title in the relevant column(s). Some of the themes are intrinsically scary or fascinating; other themes aren't wild in and of themselves, but David Lubar approaches them with twists, turns, and techniques that make them unique and impactful tales. As you build, or review, the chart, highlight the themes, and note the treatments, that interest you most as a reader or writer.

C. Commenting on his "Rumplecodespin" story, David Lubar notes that, "Fairy tales make a great starting point for getting story ideas." Pick a favorite fairy tale (or review fairy tale collections online or at the library, for inspiration). If desired, write a two- to four-page story that treats a modern-day scenario in that fairy tale's framework. As Lubar did with his story title of "Rumplecodespin," try to come up with a title that draws on the original fairy tale title, but gives it a humorous, modern spin.

D. David Lubar cites "What if . . ." questions as great inspiration for his stories. (He maintains an extensive file of "What if . . ." questions, which might offer unique jumping-off points for his short stories.) He also notes that school can be a rich source of story ideas. Discuss with friends or classmates something that you learned, or experienced, at school. Then brainstorm dark twists that could turn your personal anecdote into a great short story. Write a short story in which you apply one of the "twists" to your anecdote. As you're writing, keep in mind the features that make the stories in the *Check Out the Library Weenies* anthology so compelling. Does your story use humor (dark or otherwise), hyperbole, or irony to make a point? Is the twist truly unexpected? Are the stakes for the main character high enough? Consider drafting a letter to author David Lubar, making the case why your story could hold its own in Weenie World.

E. However complex or clever the literary devices, sources of inspiration, plot twists, or themes may be, the short-story format requires the author to "get to the heart of the matter" quickly. The author must establish character, setting, mood, tone, theme, and the story's pivotal conflict or problem in a limited amount of narrative time and space. David Lubar is a master at doing this not just efficiently, but creatively. After reading stories from this collection, try your hand at writing three or four compelling introductions (perhaps 6–10 lines of text each) that draw the reader in, and also establish all the critical story elements. If desired, pick your favorite paragraph, or "story start," and develop it into a short story.

III. Scary *and* Literary: The Art (and Craft) of the Matter

▲. Research these literary concepts and devices online or at the library:

pun; homonymic pun; connotation versus denotation; situational irony; poetic justice; point of view (including first person and third person and related variations); adage/aphorism/saying/cliché. List examples of stories from the *Check Out the Library Weenies* collection that illustrate or employ some of these devices. In pairs, or small groups, discuss how and why different literary devices (or combinations of devices) shape and drive your favorite stories from the collection.

B. "My Family History" is told from an animal (specifically a killer lizard's) perspective; "Watch Your Grammar" borrows its format from the minutes of a school board meeting. What other interesting choices does David Lubar make in stories throughout this collection? Pick your favorite story from the collection, and write a one-page essay that identifies and describes the interesting choice David Lubar made in that story; consider some of the writing challenges that choice might have presented; and think about how he handled them, as evidenced by the successful end result.

C. Author David Lubar cleverly employs word play in his stories in an ingenious layered approach. The story "Death Comes Calling" is a great illustration of this layered word play, and the interplay of words' denotations and connotations, or literal and figurative meanings. In "Death Comes Calling," the character of Death needs someone to fix his cellphone (which itself is a device used for making calls), but the author also uses the phrase "comes calling" (an old-fashioned phrase for someone coming for a visit), as well as making a phone call (the "warning call," which the victim ironically misses) the vehicle for someone's death. Inspired by "Death Comes Calling," and other cleverly layered titles in the collection, think of a pun, cliché, or popular expression, such as "A Steep Learning Curve," for example. What happens if you interpret it *literally* in a story? Brainstorm some possible phrases or words, and outline ideas for developing a story around it. If desired, write the short story.

D. Another story that plays with multiple meanings for the same word is "Watch Your Grammar," where a school experiments with giving students Grammar Watches, which give kids a small electrical shock if they make grammatical errors in their speech. David Lubar plays with the different meanings of the word "watch"—to keep an eye on, as well as an actual wristwatch—in the story's title and concept. In the story, the school decides it will explore other inventions like Posture Belts and Positive Thinking Helmets to help keep their middle school students on track. After you read the story "Watch Your Grammar," collaborate with a small group of friends or classmates to brainstorm "inventions" to address irritating habits of grown-ups, a "Longwinded Shortcutter," or whatnot. On posterboard, list name and function, and illustrate the invention. In groups, present and promote your products. Classmates can vote on best intervention invention. Use posterboard product proposals for a classroom or library display of "Intervention Inventions" inspired by David Lubar's "Watch Your Grammar" story.

E. Regarding "The Sword in the Stew," David Lubar writes: "And one of my favorite types of titles is those that play with well-known fables, classic stories, or fairy tales. In this case, *The Sword in the Stone*, which is the title of a classic book about

King Arthur, led me to "The Sword in the Stew." Do you have a favorite poem, story, or book you've read that would be fun to reimagine as, or use as the foundation for, a scary short story? What would you pick and why? Make a list of the key elements (title, main character, basic plot, and key theme) of the original work. In a second column, list how you'd change those elements to play with and transform it into your new story. What do you think might be challenging about this process?

Supports Common Core State Standards: W.4.1, 5.1, 6.1, 7.1; W.4.3, 5.3, 6.3, 7.3; SL.4.1, 5.1, 6.1, 7.1; SL.4.4, 5.4, 6.4, 7.4; RL.4.1-4, 5.1-4, 6.1-4, 7.1-4; RL.4.6, 5.6, 6.6, 7.6.

QUESTIONS FOR DISCUSSION

1. In the story "How to Slay Vampires for Fun and Profit," one vampire mocking main character Johann and his friends for being so easily tricked, says: "What fools these mortals be!" This quotes a line spoken by a character named Puck, a sprite who likes to play tricks on humans, from Shakespeare's famous play *A Midsummer Night's Dream*. Why do you think the author chooses to include the line in this story? How do some of the other stories in this collection illustrate, or explore, the idea of people facing harm, suffering, or even death, due to their own greed, ignorance, or selfishness?

2. How do the expressions "too good to be true," "the joke's on you," or "be careful what you wish for," apply to Johann in "How to Slay Vampires for Fun and Profit," the twins in "Fairyland," and the boys in "Searching for a Fart of Gold"? Are there other stories where you

would say one or all of these phrases apply? Explain your answer.

3. In his story notes referring to "All That Glitters," author David Lubar says he wanted to be sure the subgenre of "monster stories" was sufficiently represented in his anthology. How does including the element of monsters—in this case werewolves and vampires—"raise the stakes" (pun intended!) of a story? Why do you think the author chooses to have the werewolf approach another imaginary creature, a wizard, to facilitate his plan?

4. In tales like "Physics for Toons" and "Romeo, Romeo, Wherefloor Argle Roblio?", trouble with technology causes some problematic outcomes. Do you think the author is commenting in these stories on the use, or overuse, or possible downside, of so much technology in youth culture today? Why or why not? Are there other stories in the collection you might categorize as "Tech Tales"? Which ones and why?

5. Many of the tales' titles, including "Bald Truths" and "Off the Beaten Track," to name just a couple of examples, incorporate wordplay, such as puns, or are a parody of a literary reference or popular saying or phrase. Many of the titles, like "Call Me" and "I Can't Quite Put a Finger On It," work on both figurative and literal levels, making a pun and a point at the same time. If you had to pick the story title that you thought was most clever in its use of language, which one would you pick and why? Explain your answer.

6. In his story notes about "Check Out the Library Weenies," the anthology's title tale, David Lubar writes: "I was worried about going against a structure I'd established. For

the first eight books, the Weenies was someone mockable, like those joggers who never smiled, or the people
who loved their lawns a little too much. In the case of
Library Weenies, the Weenies would be the good guys."
If you have read other Weenies anthologies, how do you
feel about this change? Is your reaction positive, negative, or neutral? Explain your answer. *Check Out the
Library Weenies* celebrates the wealth of the mind, not
just the wallet. It promotes the power and pleasure of
reading, learning, science, intelligence, and invention;
but it's also a monster story, with a title that contains a
pun (since you "check out" books from your library). So
this tale exemplifies a lot of the unifying, or recurring,
structural and thematic elements that inform this anthology. Can you think of other representative elements this signature story includes? Do you agree with
the author's choice to make this the title tale? Why or
why not? If not, what tale would you pick, and why?

7. A lot of the *Check Out the Library Weenies* stories por-
tray friend, sibling, kid/parent, or kid/teacher relationships, as well as scenarios with bullies, which involve
middle-school-aged kids. Based on what you observe in
your family, school, and community, do you think that
middle school characters, attitudes, relationships, and
dynamics are depicted accurately in these stories? Why
or why not? Explain your answer, citing specific examples and stories from the anthology. Do the *Check Out
the Library Weenies* stories include some examples of
friendships where there is a good balance of power
between friends or siblings? How does the author illustrate that?

8. Several of the stories in the collection, including "Come Back Soon," "A Boy and His Frog," and "2D or Not 2D," involve characters having the power to manipulate nature, or even time or fate. Having such powers could be convenient, empowering, or even life-changing, but do you think the author is also inviting readers to think about the risks of using, or abusing, such powers? Explain your answer.

9. Urban legends are critical to "Gordie's Gonna Git Ya" and "Ghost Dancer." Does your school or community have any such legends? How, and why, do you think people keep such legends alive? In the same vein, why do you think readers enjoy scary stories?

10. The narrator in "At Stake" is excited about possessing the power to make anyone or anything "drop dead" by simply saying the words, but knows the power, which makes her different from, and a threat to, others can be a liability, too, saying: "But fear meant danger. We destroy the things we fear, if we get the chance. I'd have to watch my back." Do you agree or disagree with the idea that people destroy things they fear? What other stories in this anthology raise this idea?

11. The story "Off the Beaten Track" features a "real-life monster," a creepy man threatening to murder kids walking out by the train track. In his story notes, David Lubar says "I'm always a bit apprehensive when I use a story with a real-life monster rather than an imaginary creature. But I think my readers can handle this one." Do you find this kind of story, or the stories with make-believe monsters, like werewolves or vampires, scarier? If you were the author or editor on this project, would you have chosen to include this story, or would you have left it out in favor of a fictitious monster story?

Supports Common Core State Standards: RL.4.1-4, 5.1-4, 6.1-4, 7.1-4; RL.4.6, 5.6, 6.6, 7.6; SL.4.1, 5.1, 6.1, 7.1; SL.4.4, 5.4, 6.4, 7.4.

Read on for a sneak peek of
David Lubar's new novel,
coming soon from Starscape

When seventh grader Nicholas V. Landrew, his beloved pet gerbil Henrietta, and a package of ground beef are beamed aboard an alien space ship, they soon find themselves on the run in a madcap chase across the universe.

Now all Nicholas wants to do is get back home before his parents find out and ground him forever, but with the Universal Police hot on his trail, that won't be easy. Before it's all over, Henrietta will find herself safely ensconced back in her cage, Nicholas will be crowned Emperor of the Universe, and something even more surprising will happen to the package of ground beef.

GONE IN A FLASH

Nicholas V. Landrew was not a typical ninth grader. That isn't surprising. There is no typical ninth grader. Or tenth or eighth. Or teacher or parent. Or rodeo clown or oyster shucker, for that matter. But Nicholas was not far from what was considered *normal* by the social standards of his place and time, or the hypercritical judgment of his peers. He couldn't shoot milk from the corner of his eye, like Nikolai C. Landrew of Oxnard, MI, dousing candles at ten feet, or memorize the serial number of a dollar bill on sight and extract the square root to seventeen decimal places, like Nicole D. Landrew of Harrisburg, Pennsylvania. On the other hand, neither Nikolai nor Nicole would ever rule the universe, so we will not speak of them again.

Nicholas V. Landrew lived in Yelm, Washington with his family. Though, at the moment, he was home alone. Nicholas's father, who bore a strong resemblance to a bearded John Lennon, and his mother, who bore a startling resemblance to a young and beardless Paul McCartney, formed two fourths of a Beatles Tribute/Parody group called *The Beegles*. They wore beagle masks and sang songs with titles like "I Wanna Shake Your Paw," "While My Guitar Gently Barks," and "Yellow Snow Submarine." (If you find yourself wondering why look-alikes would wear masks, you are not alone. Mr. and Mrs. Landrew, while highly creative, fun loving, and musically talented, were not deep thinkers. They could have used a good manager.) Despite their hopes of capturing the lucrative teen market, their core base of fans were mostly not even pre-teens but pre-pre-teens in the four-to-six age range. The Beegles were currently on tour in Australia, but kept in touch with Nicholas through lengthy voicemails, to which he responded with brief texts. They rarely communicated directly, unless they were in the same room. And not always, even then. Mr. and Mrs. Landrew do not play a major role in what is to come. Beagle faces, on the other hand, do. As do managers. But let's not get ahead of ourselves.

As for Nicholas's face, he shared his parents' dark hair, which he liked to keep cut fairly short. He had his father's narrow nose and his mother's soulful eyes, making him more attractive than he realized. He was one minor growth spurt away from his adult height, which would put him slightly above average. He weighed no more than ten pounds above average weight for his age, according to the height-weight chart in his doctor's office, which seemed to be designed for assessing the health of skeletons and scarecrows.

It is just as well the elder Landrews were absent. Nicholas had been slapped with a two-week suspension for bringing a light saber to school. It wasn't a real weapon. It was made of the sort of soft plastic that could do about as much harm to a living creature as a Whiffle bat. He'd only brought it because he thought the battery-operated whoosh it made would sound awesome in the empty gym. But the rules against bringing weapons to school were rigid. Given that the suspension ended the day before the start of spring break, Nicholas was basically facing three weeks free of the classroom. That was fine with him. He was a bit of a loner. And he was struggling a little with algebra, despite it being his favorite class of all time. Worst of all, he was flunking French, which was definitely his least favorite class of all time, past, present, and probably future. (The past, present, and future of French verbs being a huge part of his problem with that language.) While we have little interest in Nicholas's family, or his education, Nicholas's gerbil was another matter. Nicholas loved Henrietta. He could talk to her without being judged, and look her in the eye without feeling uncomfortable or awkward. This made her unique among his acquaintances.

Then, Henrietta vanished.

Poof! (A sound that never, in the entire history of vanishings, has ever actually been made. An authentic vanishing sound, created as air rushed in to fill the void, would be more along the lines of *schwupf* or *fwomph*.)

Had Nicholas not been there to see the laser-bright flash of purple light that accompanied Henrietta's disappearance, he naturally would have assumed she'd flattened her body enough to escape beneath the door of her cage and then scrambled off in search of greener pastures. Or, at least, greener nuggets of gerbil chow. Nicholas might have searched and mourned. He might even have created a "lost gerbil" poster and papered the neighborhood with copies, enhancing the local suspicion among some of the more elderly residents that there was something just a little bit odd about that Landrew boy. But he never would have known Henrietta had been abducted by alien scientists.

After staring at the empty cage for a period, as if an unexplained disappearance might magically become balanced by an unexplained appearance (along with a resounding *foop*), Nicholas slid the door of the cage up, reached through the opening, and explored the bedding. He noticed a warmth to the cedar shavings right at the spot where he'd last seen Henrietta. Fortunately, it was a dry warmth. Though far from omniscient, Nicholas was highly intuitive. On a hunch, he went to his kitchen, extracted a four-pound family-size package of vacuum-sealed fresh-ground hamburger meat from the refrigerator, and placed it in the cage, directly on top of the warm spot.

Nicholas waited. He didn't have to wait long. That's fortunate, given Nicholas's short-to-moderate-length attention span. In another moment or two, had nothing happened, he would have begun to question his intuition, and returned the meat to the refrigerator. But before doubt could lead to action, the meat disappeared in an identical laser-bright flash of purple light.

"Roach brains!" Nicholas exclaimed, blinking against the yellow after-image that had painted his field of view. The origin of this phrase as his favorite expression of surprise and/or dismay is tied to a catastrophically disastrous science-fair project he attempted in 5th grade, and is best left undescribed beyond that, for now.

"I'm coming, Henrietta," Nicholas said. He pictured himself bravely leaping into a raging river to rescue his gerbil, or commandeering a passing motorcycle to give chase to the unmarked white van that had abducted her. (Abduction vans in Nicholas's heroic rescue fantasies were virtually always white, and passing motorcyclists were inevitably generous about allowing unlicensed youths to borrow their wheels for reckless ventures.) Having no such river from which to pluck Henrietta, or van to pursue, Nicholas contemplated placing his hand where the gerbil and the hamburger meat had been. But the image of his hand disappearing in a flash of laser-bright purple light while the rest of him remained in his room sickened him as much as his 5th grade science-fair project had sickened numerous classmates, three teachers, two administrators, and one custodian who was definitely working in the wrong field.

Nicholas unlatched the top of the cage, lifted it up on its hinges, and stepped inside. His feet barely fit. *Maybe this is a bad idea*, he thought, as the handless image was replaced with a footless one. He stared down at his shoes just in time to catch the laser-bright purple flash of light enveloping his body.

FOR MORE WILD AND WACKY
WEENIES TALES
CHECK OUT

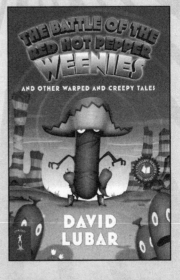

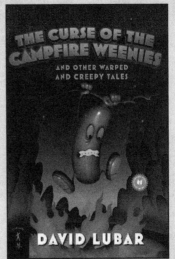

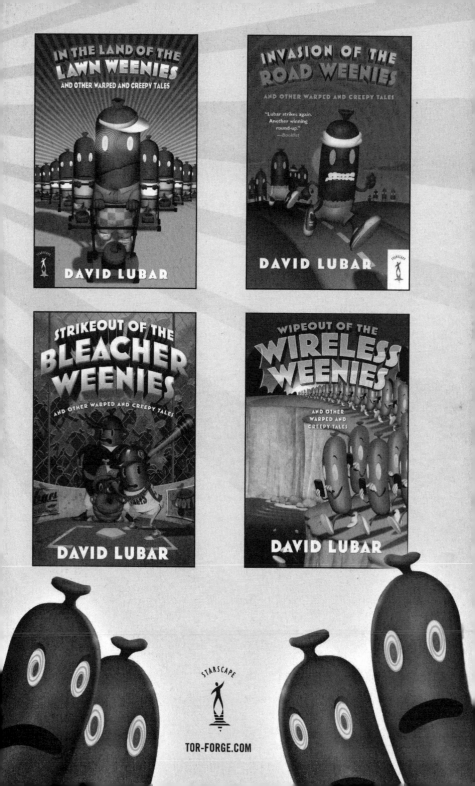

ABOUT THE AUTHOR

David Lubar grew up in Morristown, New Jersey. His books include the acclaimed novels *Hidden Talents*, *True Talents*, and *Flip*; the popular Nathan Abercrombie, Accidental Zombie series; and the bestselling Weenies short-story collections. He lives in Nazareth, Pennsylvania. You can visit him on the web at www.davidlubar.com.